TINY VICES

TINY VICES

A NOVEL

LINDA DAHL

swp

SHE WRITES PRESS

Copyright © 2025 Linda Dahl

All rights reserved. No part of this publication may be reproduced, distributed, or transmitted in any form or by any means, including photocopying, recording, digital scanning, or other electronic or mechanical methods, without the prior written permission of the publisher, except in the case of brief quotations embodied in critical reviews and certain other noncommercial uses permitted by copyright law. For permission requests, please address She Writes Press.

Published 2025
Printed in the United States of America
Print ISBN: 978-1-64742-930-0
E-ISBN: 978-1-64742-931-7
Library of Congress Control Number: [LOCCN]

For information, address:
She Writes Press
1569 Solano Ave #546
Berkeley, CA 94707

Interior Design by Andrea Reider

She Writes Press is a division of SparkPoint Studio, LLC.

Company and/or product names that are trade names, logos, trademarks, and/or registered trademarks of third parties are the property of their respective owners and are used in this book for purposes of identification and information only under the Fair Use Doctrine.

This is a work of fiction. Names, characters, places, and incidents either are the product of the author's imagination or are used fictitiously. Any resemblance to actual persons, living or dead, is entirely coincidental.

NO AI TRAINING: Without in any way limiting the author's [and publisher's] exclusive rights under copyright, any use of this publication to "train" generative artificial intelligence (AI) technologies to generate text is expressly prohibited. The author reserves all rights to license uses of this work for generative AI training and development of machine learning language models.

Tiny vices are habitual and usually trivial defects or shortcomings. Think of a venial (slight, forgivable) sin versus a mortal (lethal, unpardonable) sin.

Sometime in the Spring of 1986

Spring break in Mexico at Rincón Bay began predictably enough. Nineteen-year-old Kathy Talley hit the beach, and when she started to feel sunburned, she dozed under an umbrella with a book she didn't open. Later she and some of the other girls staying at the hostel went to a bar and got sloshed.

The next day there was a party on a sailboat. Despite being hungover, Kathy freely indulged in weed and margaritas. That night, she collapsed onto her narrow bed at the hostel and slept until noon the next day, when she got up and had breakfast, then walked around the little town, buying cheap souvenirs and a cotton tunic embroidered with flowers.

The third night was the last, when they had a humongous beach party with a bonfire, live band, and all you could drink for five dollars. Kathy wore the flowered tunic over her bikini and got wasted. As she was puking in the sand sometime later, a random girl handed her tissues and a bottle of water. She

VIII   TINY VICES

even tried to help Kathy get the vomit stains off her blouse, before they both collapsed with laughter. Jenny, was it? Jan? A name that started with J anyway, a big girl with purple-tipped hair and a whooping laugh.

The two of them walked—stumbling mostly—away from the party up the beach toward a big rock tower near the cliffs at the end. Sand in their clothes, in their hair. Later, Kathy would remember thinking her new tunic must be ruined already. The moonlight that kept punching through a scrum of cloud cover lent the scene a mysterious air, like an old Hitchcock movie. Spooky and quiet.

After that . . . but she didn't want to remember.

PART ONE

Spring 2016

The call, the kind Kathy had learned to dread, came that morning when, for once, she had a chunk of time free to paint or just putter. She left a note for Bernard, canceled her afternoon classes, and headed across town.

She found her sister on the patio. One leg was bandaged and there was a mean scrape above her right elbow. She looked a little pale but otherwise fine.

Kathy sat beside her and took her hand. "What happened, Corina?"

"Oh!" Corina said, looking up with a little gasp. "It's you!"

"Imalia called and said you took a fall, so I wanted to come over."

Corina frowned. "Well, I tripped or something. She made me go to urgent care." She pointed at the bandage on her leg and shook her head. "How did that get there?"

"Well, they had to treat the cuts, you know. Imalia said she found you face down out here."

"I was just walking around in the backyard!"

"Do you feel all right now?"

"Yes. All this *fuss*." Corina rolled her eyes.

In the scheme of things in Corina's life now, this fall was turning out to be a one, barely a blip. *But you never know*, Kathy thought.

Corina peered at her sister in that feline way she now did sometimes, eyes narrowed and empty. "Why are you here?"

Kathy flinched. "To make sure you're okay!" Oh dear, she was cranky too. *Breathe. Exhale. Repeat.* Calmly, she said, "And now that I'm here, let's have lunch and catch up."

"But why didn't Becca come?"

Besides the fact that she has that crisis with Cam going on? "She's at work, remember? At the craft shop? But she'll come over tonight, I think."

Imalia had said during their earlier conversation that she was worried about Corina's balance. *Another doctor appointment. They are endless.* Now she appeared with a tray of Corina's sushi—the only thing she'd eat—a sandwich for Kathy, and a pitcher of iced tea.

"Isn't this nice," Kathy said. "But why are we sitting outside?" The Arizona heat was stupefying, despite the shades on the patio and the huge fan.

Corina raised her eyebrows and sighed. "Because I need to find Henrique."

"What? The turtle?"

"He's a tortoise! That's why I tripped. I was in the scrub, trying to find him. He hides. I haven't seen him in, oh, well, a while at least. I hope he's in a tunnel."

Ah yes, Corina lived in fear of a coyote or raven swooping up her last remaining pet. She had always been surrounded by animals—dogs, cats, birds, even insects—but she no longer had the capacity to care for herself, let alone pets. So, Henrique, check.

Corina reached for a piece of sushi and stuffed it in her mouth haphazardly. She patted an old photo album that was open on the table. "I was looking at the family. When we went to Maine. How old were we?"

"That summer?" Kathy swallowed a bite of tuna. "I think I was like, twelve, so you would have been ten."

"Look at us, we look so *happy*. Even little Pete. See?" She tapped one of the photos. "Holding up a little fish he caught, so proud."

"Those family reunions. Remember Gramma in that swimsuit that came down to her knees?"

They both giggled; then Corina began crying. Slowly, as if her heart was breaking. "I don't go anywhere now. I'm lonely," she said in a small voice. "I never see anybody."

Here we go again. "That's not true. I'm here."

"But then you leave me."

"But you have your friends. The kids."

"They never call me."

Kathy mentally rolled her eyes. She reminded herself for the thousandth time that it was pointless to argue when Corina got upset. It was part of the disease. She couldn't help the mood swings and the memory gaps.

"I want to go somewhere," Corina said suddenly. "I used to go everywhere!"

"Yes, you did." Around the world. Business class, whatever that meant. Kathy wouldn't know. When *she* flew, it was in the cattle-car section.

"I want all of us to be together. You, me, Becca. A family trip, like we used to do."

"I suppose we could go somewhere. Taos, maybe? Or, I don't know, the beach?" As soon as the words were out of her mouth, Kathy wanted to kick herself. Not Rincón Bay! Now that Corina couldn't deal with airports it was the only feasible beach within driving distance. Rincón Bay. The town Kathy had always refused to go back to.

Her sister's eyes lit up. "Oh, the beach! Yes!"

"Or how about the mountains?" Kathy suggested hastily, trying to redirect.

"No, the beach! Oh, we've got to—before I'm stuck here forever." Corina's cat eyes were filling with tears. "I know I'm going to forget everything soon." She sniffed. "I need a happy time."

Oh God. "Sure, yes, we'll do something special. You, me, Becca. And Pete. We can't leave Pete out."

"No!" Corina jerked back in her chair. "Not Pete."

"But he could use a break too. He's got his kidney problem, his liver . . . A lot to deal with . . . And he never goes anywhere. If we figure out a schedule where he won't miss a treatment, we should ask him along."

"Oh, well, if we have to. Do you know, I was thinking about it—when was it, today, my beach house on Catalina? We could go there! I miss the ocean so much. It's so hot here. Like a furnace." Corina's eyes widened. "Or, I know! That nice hotel in Cabo!" She had perked up now.

"Both of them are too far to drive." Kathy didn't bother to add that Corina's ex-husband, Tom, was now living in the Catalina house, so that was out. And "that nice hotel in Cabo" would cost a fortune. It would have to be Rincón Bay or nothing.

Doctor Anne Maples had been chipping away at Kathy's fear, as therapists were trained to do. Or rather, nudging Kathy to chip away at it. Or take a sledgehammer to it: go back to the place of fear and loathing and face it down. *It, it, it.* Her stubbornness about not going to the only beach a reasonable drive away from Tucson and her silence about why she wouldn't do so had been a perennial irritant between her and Bernard. *Okay, Anne, you win, I'll do it. I don't want to. But I'll do it. I can avoid the part of the beach where* . . . Kathy took a deep breath. *Where it happened.* She pictured her therapist's face smiling encouragement at her.

"Look, Corina, we can get to Rincón Bay in a few hours."

"Okay then." Corina flapped her hands suddenly. "Look, a *Lucifer!*" She pointed at one of the bird feeders dotted around her large, beautifully landscaped backyard with the rarely used pool gleaming in the center.

"Lucifer?"

"That hummer over there. You hardly ever see Lucifers in these parts. That purple throat! And see how he's hunched over? Oh, my," Corina sighed, "my day is complete. We're going to the beach and I've seen a beautiful Lucifer. I'm going to go to bed now."

"What?" Startled, Kathy spoke loudly and the oddly named hummingbird darted away.

"For a nap." Corina glanced at her as if to say, *You're a little slow on the uptake.*

Kathy sighed. "I need to get going anyway. I'll talk to Becca and Pete about Rincón Bay."

"But you hate Rincón Bay," Corina pointed out unexpectedly.

"I don't. I just haven't wanted to go back there."

Corina picked at the cashmere shawl that she insisted on wearing even in the heat. "You were so . . . what's the word? I can't . . . When you came back from there. You were *remote*," she decided.

"Was I? It's so long ago, I don't remember." Kathy stood up and gave her sister a hug, feeling her bird-wing shoulders tremble slightly—evidence of the recent diagnosis of Parkinson's. On top of everything else. *Damn.*

"Where are you going?"

"To teach a class."

"Oh."

They went inside, where Corina promptly headed for her spot, the old recliner in the den, the smallest room in the sprawling house. She closed her eyes. Imalia appeared with a blanket and a glass of ice water.

Kathy leaned over her sister's drooping head and kissed it. "Bye, Corina. Bye, Imalia."

In the car, Kathy blasted the air conditioning. She had parked in the shade, which made a tiny but important difference once the temperature went over a hundred. She slumped behind the wheel as the cold air fought its puny way through the heat, feeling the rush of despair she always felt after she was with Corina now. What was the name of that book about cancer? She'd seen it destroy her mother.

The Emperor of All Maladies, that was it.

Corina had probably had Alzheimer's for years. Maybe, given what Kathy had read in an online article from the Mayo Clinic, for decades. At first gradually and then rapidly, she was more anxious, hypersensitive, and what their mother would have called "flighty." Her getting lost in the Atlanta airport, one of the world's busiest, had led to what must have been an epic meltdown as it resulted in an involuntary overnight stay in a hospital until Tom collected her the next day. After that, a round of doctors and tests and, eventually, the diagnosis.

If, Kathy thought, cancer was the emperor, then Alzheimer's was God Almighty...

Two days later, Kathy and Becca decided to splurge. Instead of a cheap lunch at a taqueria or fast-food place, they met at Mirabel's, usually beyond both their budgets. At Becca's suggestion, they sat on the patio instead of in the air-conditioned dining room because it was much quieter outdoors. The lush plants and splashing Mexican-tiled fountain gave at least the illusion of coolness.

Becca did not love Kathy's idea about the trip and she made no effort to hide that fact; almost immediately, they started arguing. Gone were the days when Kathy could order her little sister around. As the youngest, Becca had grown a tough hide.

Their waitperson, a college student with a badge marked "Kim," handed them their menus with a smile and recited the specials before staging a rapid retreat.

"Come on, don't be like this," Kathy said, changing tack.

"Like what?"

"You know. Stubborn. Obstinate."

"Me?" Becca put a hand to her heart. "Well, there's the pot calling the kettle black. No, but really? Mexico? All four of us? It's completely impractical. For one thing."

But Kathy had that expression on her face, and when she looked like that, it was usually game over. Becca knew Kathy would have rehearsed the reasons and possible rebuttals for this trip like a lawyer preparing for a trial. And also like a lawyer, she often had another, hidden agenda. Ostensibly she was arguing for the four siblings to get together for what they all knew (though no one was about to say it) would be the last time. A reprise of all those trips in their childhood and reluctant adolescence when the whole extended family got together. Not high-end resorts—those came later—just motels near nice lakes and beaches and mountain spots, heaven for kids and a chance for teens to sneak off and grown-ups to relax. Those were the times when their parents were at ease, especially their mother, Julia, who worried about them so much and most of all, of course, about their father. All of them noticed how quiet, subdued Ward, usually cloistered in his den with his martinis, became an outgoing, card-playing funnyman when they were away from home and surrounded by relatives. His demons seeming to have fled, his children fluttered around him in a way they never did at home, and Julia relaxed with her beloved bridge games, battling over the cards with the kin.

And Kathy's trump card—Becca sensed that she was about to play it—was that it was the tenth anniversary of their mother's death (Ward had died seven years before her). It would have made Julia so glad to see her children all together.

Kathy wasn't about to tell her sister this part, but really the push for the trip was down to Anne Maples. Becca knew—if she remembered—that Kathy saw, or had seen, a therapist (as didn't pretty much everybody these days, anyway?). But Becca wouldn't remember that awful time for Kathy after spring break in Rincón Bay. She'd only been ten or eleven. So long ago now.

Then a sophomore in college, Kathy had stopped going to classes at the University of Arizona after she got back from Mexico, showing up only to take her finals. She would have flunked out if her grades before hadn't been so good up to then. Then she'd gone back East for the summer to her childhood home, staying mostly in her room except for meals and watching TV, refusing to get a job or even see old friends from high school. Julia had fluttered around her, Ward had sputtered, but Kathy wouldn't talk to them. She didn't even tell Corina what had happened during spring break.

Now, thirty years later, and a year and a half, finally, in therapy with Dr. "Call me Anne" Maples, she was going to go back to the place that had been secretly obsessing her for far too long. But Becca didn't need to know that. She just needed to agree to the trip.

Kathy had said to Anne at their latest therapy session, "I've been looking in the *DSM-5*." The latest version of *The Diagnostic and Statistical Manual of Mental Disorders*; she'd gone to the central library downtown and found it in the reference section. Anne cocked her head. "Oh? And?"

"I find some aspects of the diagnosis terrifying."

"Remember I said it's more of a guideline? Just a guideline, Kathy. Certain traits of counterphobia. At the low end of the spectrum." She paused. "But did reading it give you any clarity?"

"It did. Like why I have to help people in scary situations. I guess maybe it is a kind of compulsion." All the protests, the trips into cartel territory with Border Aid, the domestic abuse casualties, the substance-use-disorder kids.

"'Counterphobia,'" Anne read from her own *DSM-5*. "'A compulsion to seek out the causes of anxiety instead of avoiding them.'" She set down the heavy book. "But I like another definition better. Here it is." She read from a paper: "'Instead of fleeing the source of fear, the individual actively seeks it out in the hope of overcoming the original anxiousness.' Hope. I like that. How well do you think this definition describes you?" Her face was flat, wiped clean of her nearly habitual Cheshire cat grin.

"You're the expert," Kathy said. "Does it?"

Anne smiled at this obvious attempt at manipulation. "Isn't there a difference between helping people in trouble and compulsively seeking out danger?" she asked gently.

Anne rarely made a declarative statement.

Always lobbing it back to me, Kathy thought.

"Well, then you'd think I'd *want* to go back to that place that . . . well, *you* know, got me in trouble. But I've always resisted it. Okay, I know, I know, I've substituted other things for going there and confronting . . . it. So weird that *Rincón Bay* is the *one place* I can think of for a last trip with my family."

"Is it, though? Weird?"

Kathy sighed. "Yeah, okay. It's like my unconscious set me up."

Now, at the restaurant with Becca, she could hardly believe that she was lobbying so hard for this trip that she only half wanted to go on—yet she was determined to see it through.

"It seems risky, hauling Pete down there in his condition." Becca frowned.

"Well, I talked to his nephrologist. If we go on a Friday afternoon after he's had dialysis and are back in Tucson Monday afternoon for his next session, he said it would be okay."

"But Corina? She's so fragile too."

"Well, she complains all the time about being lonely and bored. I mean, this trip was her idea. She loves the ocean. And Imalia can come along to help. Becca, if there's ever going to be a time for us to get together, it's *now*. Before..."

She waved a hand and forced a smile. She was feeling a little sick, dizzy. She and Becca had gone on a hike before lunch. *Too much sun on the hike?* But she knew. It was looming: that cheapo, all-inclusive, three-day spring break in 1986. She had been a wild child, had recently been dumped by her boyfriend and had been ready to party. Maybe find some hot guy...

Well.

"I just don't know when there will be another chance for us to do something together," she said quietly, recovering.

"You never wanted to go there before when the kids were little."

"No. But now I do. And let's face it, you could use a break." Kathy took a long drink of her iced tea. Becca—Sweet-and-Sour, as Kathy thought of her—had been going through hell with her son, Cam. This trip might not be the kind of vacation she had hoped for, but at least it would be a chance to get away.

Becca forked a piece of chicken from her salad and chewed. She felt cornered. Kathy had sprung the idea of this "family reunion" while they were resting under a mesquite tree halfway through their prelunch hike in Sabino Canyon. Reminding Becca how much fun they'd had going away as a family (she assumed Becca had had fun, playing with her own gang), how much Julia and Ward had come into their own at those lodges and cabins with the grandparents, aunts, uncles, cousins. (Where were all those people now? Becca mused. Dispersed around the globe, the cousins in Thailand, London, San Francisco. Or dead? The old folks were, of course.)

"Well?" Kathy prodded.

"I'm thinking," Becca said, switching from salad to scoops of the excellent guac with the super-organic blue corn chips. She could feel Kathy watching her eat with her usual irritation. She felt bad for her older sister: no matter how much Becca and Corina stuffed themselves, neither ever gained a pound, whereas Kathy had only to look at food to put on weight.

"Okay! We'll go to Rincón Bay." Becca stabbed again at something in her salad bowl.

Kathy clapped her hands together. "It's settled then!" She glanced at her watch. "Oops, I gotta go or I'll be late for class." Kathy rummaged in her bag for her wallet.

"The new one? At that bar? How's it going?"

"Today's the first class! Wish me luck."

"It's on me," Becca said, mentally wincing. "Go."

Kathy stood up and produced a twenty-dollar bill. "Here, sweetie! This should cover it. Sorry to rush, Bec." She came around the table and folded her arms around her sister. "Love you."

"Yeah, me too. Go."

Kathy hurried off. She was always late.

Seconds later, the bill came. Kathy's half was thirty-eight dollars.

Typical, Becca thought, *and it couldn't come at a worse time.* Not when the cost of rehab for her seventeen-year-old son loomed. She slapped down her credit card, blinking hard.

CHAPTER 2

Pete wasn't answering his phone again. After she finished teaching her Intro to Feminist Art class at the community college, Kathy resigned herself to driving across town in rush-hour traffic to check on him. He was probably sleeping, but there was always a chance of some disaster. A few weeks ago, she'd stopped by when he wasn't picking up and found him lying on the floor of the bathroom, confused and with a bleeding cut to his forehead. She'd taken him to the ER, where they'd said he was just dehydrated.

After she rang the doorbell of his apartment several times, she let herself in with her key. The place wasn't as disorderly as usual, so the cleaner that she, Becca, and Corina (well, mostly Corina) paid for, along with everything else, must have been there recently.

"Pete! Pete?"

No answer.

Please don't be lying on the bedroom or the bathroom floor. Yet she couldn't help being annoyed when she found him in the small spare bedroom that was his "studio," headphones on, shaking his head ecstatically.

"You know how much he loves his music," Corina had reminded her when Kathy argued against getting him a two-bedroom apartment after they'd finally pried him out of the increasingly dangerous trailer park he'd been living in.

"A studio would be fine," Becca said, siding with Kathy.

"A palace!" Kathy added, knowing it was a gratuitous comment and not very nice. But then, Pete had a way of making you not want to be nice.

Corina had said she'd cover two-thirds of the rent, so that was that. He got the two-bedroom apartment, the poky second bedroom crammed with speakers, tweeters, and other expensive-looking equipment, probably all bought hot. With their money.

At least he's too frail now to steal anything, Kathy thought, watching her brother before he noticed her in the doorway.

Pete could be the poster boy—poster codger, to be accurate—for addicts who somehow survive past their sell-by date was her next thought as she waved at her brother to get his attention. Pete was like a broken-down cowboy (had he ever even ridden a horse?), or no, like Keith Richards without the glam. A walking cautionary tale. Well, when had decrepitude ever stopped substance-use-disorder people? She knew most of the PC vocab around addiction, tried to be au courant about it. Indeed—prodded by Becca—she'd attended a few 12-step meetings for family and friends, picked up some lingo, read some pamphlets. And she tried not to judge Pete, but that was an uphill task. Becca, a regular Al-Anon attendee, said stuff like

Of course you have good reasons for hating substances, Kath: look at Dad and his martini catatonia. And how "enabled" Pete had been by Julia. Still and all, Kathy couldn't help but feel gratified when even Becca would get fed up with their brother.

Pete finally noticed her standing there and—typical—self-importantly motioned her to wait—what, was he in the grip of some sublime composition? Nobody had ever heard his tunes, but it didn't stop him from claiming he had a body of work—or "shitload of tunes," as he put it. Kathy rolled her eyes and sighed.

After Julia had succumbed to cancer, the Talley sisters had inherited more modest sums than they'd expected. That was, they knew, thanks to Pete, who Julia had carried except for his brief intervals of independence. And inheriting the responsibility for Pete meant fighting with Pete, threatening to cut him off, banning him from their homes, and, of course, spending much of their inheritance on him. At last, too sick to get wasted, he'd quit whatever drugs he'd been on —they were never sure just what they were besides booze, the old faithful. Two years ago, they got him this apartment, close to the dialysis center.

The fact that Kathy and Corina were six and four years older than Pete respectively hadn't stopped him from terrorizing them when they were kids. Becca, two years younger, had naturally borne the brunt of his merciless teasing, especially about what he called her kinky hair. Once, in a temper, he'd winged a fork at her head, just missing her and gouging a wall. Another time, when Kathy was babysitting, he'd smashed his fist through a window in a rage and she had to take him to the emergency room in a cab, with Becca and Corina cowering beside her. He'd laughed at Kathy for being fat, Corina for being skinny. He'd stolen their babysitting money. He'd stolen from Julia's wallet. He'd gotten sent to juvie while Kathy and Becca were away at college, and after he got out he was caught breaking and entering two streets down from their house. A county sheriff's deputy had shown up and given him two options: go to jail or get out of town. It had felt like some old, nightmarish Western.

Pete had gone to LA with one of his questionable friends but unsurprisingly turned up on the Talley doorstep months later, broke and exhausted. Julia had taken him in (ignoring the sheriff, who probably couldn't enforce his ban anyway), fed him his favorite meals, bought him clothes, gave him money. Their father, Ward, lectured him in his den, discussions that turned into shouting matches before Ward would order Pete to leave, then slam the door and presumably mix an extra-strong martini.

And yet Pete had a "good" side. There were times when he helped with chores, held a reasonably intelligent conversation, bought Christmas presents, joined in a game of Scrabble. But you could never count on the good times. And nothing about him was ever entirely clear. Was he mentally ill? If so, what was his diagnosis? Was he straight, gay? Did (how did) he earn enough money to scrape by, apart from Julia's frequent handouts?

Now here he was, cirrhotic, severely diabetic, and if the sisters hadn't supported him, he'd be sleeping on cardboard. *Or dead*, Kathy thought grimly as she sat waiting on a giant speaker that had to have cost a good portion of her yearly salary teaching art classes as an adjunct. But of course, none of his gear was retail.

"It's a wrap," he said eventually. Removing the headphones, he smiled at Kathy mischievously.

She couldn't get used to this smiling. It made her nervous. Yet she had to admit, he was oddly more cheerful now that his kidneys and liver were shot.

Twiddling with some dials, he said, "What can I do you for?"

What can you do me for? Kathy thought. *That's rich.* "Well, I came by because you didn't . . ." Then she had a better idea. "To tell you about a plan Becca, Corina, and I came up with."

"Uh-oh."

"All good, Pete! Listen, wouldn't it be great for the four of us to go on a trip together? A long weekend at the beach. Swim, get on a boat, eat fresh fish." She showed him the website of the small hotel she'd picked out—the price was right—on her phone. Palm trees and a low, whitewashed building.

He scratched his chin. "Guess I better check with the doc first."

But Kathy could tell he was excited.

"Mm, I already talked to him. It's cool as long as you don't miss a session. So we can leave on a Friday afternoon and be back Monday afternoon. Sound good?"

"We're driving? So you mean Rincón Bay, right? Man, I haven't been there in a coon's age. Corina's coming too?"

"The four of us, yep."

"But Corina's . . . you know."

"She really wants to do this. Remember those family reunions we used to go to?"

"All the cousins." Pete chuckled. "Wonder what happened to them. Didn't what's-her-name, Annie, join a cult?"

"She became a Baha'i. Hardly a cult."

"Close enough." He smirked. "And what's-his-name, Carl? The cousin from Montana? He's Tina now. Facebook."

"Give it a rest! And, um, while I'm here . . ." Kathy peered at him. "Wait, do you have that Life Alert thing on?" Pete had given her power of attorney awhile back. She took the responsibility seriously.

"I wear it at night." Seeing her expression, he added, "I'm *on it*, Kathy."

"But I noticed when I came in that the lockbox for the alert hasn't been set up." For weeks, she'd been trying to get Pete to install the frigging thing outside his door so if there was an "incident," emergency responders could code it in instead of smashing his door down.

"Haven't got to that yet."

"Well, I'm here now, so let's do it."

"I don't need your help."

"'Course you don't." The essence of Pete: I Need Help, Leave Me Alone. "Let's just get this done."

"All right, all right, I have to find the thing first."

Kathy went to his tiny living room and waited again, this time on what had been Mom's couch, old and lumpy now. The only other furnishing of note was the giant TV screen.

Pete made a show of rummaging through piles.

"Got it," he said at last.

After they set it up, which took maybe ten minutes, he flopped into his recliner as if this small chore had exhausted him.

"I'm gonna take a nap," he said.

Kathy got him a glass of water.

Pete drank it down in one go. "I'm doing pretty good. Just get a little tired, you know."

"Yeah. All that working on your music."

"Doin' pretty good," he repeated. As if saying it would make it so. "Bring it on!" He looked at her and smiled. "I'm down with it. Whatever. Nothin' botherin' me." He continued to smile.

Kathy left, shutting the door softly behind her. Pete's odd smile creeped her out.

But Pete didn't go to sleep. He watched the white-hot afternoon sun pierce the slats of the Venetian blinds and started to feel that itch as the sun started to lower, that now-or-never time for an addict. There were oxies a doctor had prescribed for his back in the kitchenette, behind some cans on a shelf.

In a minute.

He thought about Rincón Bay. The time he'd gone down there with Mom and Dad. They'd stayed at a fancy resort. He played nine holes with the old man, then they sat drinking martinis together in the clubhouse. Went out on a boat another day. Drank a lot of beer. Mom dressed up for dinner every night at the resort restaurant. Pearls, the whole nine yards. He'd felt like he was in a bad play, per usual with the parents. Had to bust out, get to the part of the town where things were happening. He stirred, shook his head. Maybe he'd get up now and take a pill, okay, two, but that was the limit. He was good about it now, not greedy anymore. Then he'd microwave one of those renal-friendly frozen dinners the meal service delivered every week, and he'd watch a show. Man, it was gonna be good to get out of this place.

CHAPTER 3

"**I**'ve got something to tell you," Kathy said to Bernard when she got home after seeing Pete.

"Uh-oh." Her husband set down his book, which, glancing at it, she saw without surprise was yet another jazz biography. He looked at her. "Okay, what?"

She sat down across from him. "Becca and Corina and I—and Pete—have decided to go away, just a long weekend. A family vacation. Um, to the beach. Rincón Bay." She paused. "We can't fly, obviously."

Bernard frowned. "Rincón Bay, you? And is that a good idea?"

They were sitting on their deck behind the townhouse. Bernard poured more lemonade into their glasses from the pitcher—they had recently decided to cut back, not drink booze until the evening. He took a long swallow. "Well, Corina, *maybe*. But Pete? He's got every damn thing wrong with him you can have."

"His doctor says it's okay, as long as he's back for dialysis Monday afternoon. So..."

He shook his head. "I could never get you to go there on a *family vacation*. You said it creeped you out."

"I know. But." Kathy stood up, signaling the end of the conversation. Otherwise, they would get into an argument.

But Bernard kept on as she began to walk away. "You *hate* that place."

She whirled around. "I did hate it. But, well, it's all in the past now. And it's our last chance to get together like we always did when we were kids. Before. You know . . . Corina really wants to go to a beach."

Bernard drummed his fingers on his knee. "I don't get you, Kathy. Why should you let her decide where you go? Go to a resort, get a massage. She's got the money."

"Can we not talk about this anymore?"

He shook his head again. "The kids *begged* us to go there. Everybody went there. All their friends. Ours. But nope, Kathy won't budge. It's 110 in the fucking shade, but hey, she won't talk about it."

"I said I was sorry, Bernard. I am. Sorry."

"Yup. Anyway, it's time to go rattle the pots and pans."

Cooking always put Bernard in a good, or at least a better, mood.

That night, the menu was pozole—Bernard had found a new recipe online the other day—and his signature salad, followed by pineapple flan.

"Delicious as usual," Kathy said as she carried the dishes to the sink. "I am a lucky woman."

Draining his wine glass, Bernard leaned against the counter and circled back to the trip. "I mean, is it wise? Two sick people? A long car trip? To Mexico?"

Kathy slapped the sponge on the counter. "Bernard, can we please, *please* not discuss it? We want to do this trip. Corina and Pete . . . it's probably our last time to all be together. And again, there's only one drivable beach." She bent over the sink and started scrubbing. "And maybe it's a good thing for me to go there. Dr. Maples thinks so," she added, her voice dropping.

Bernard set down his wine glass. *Leave it*, he thought. As long as he'd known her, Kathy had gone her own way. Paid her own way through grad school with waitressing, babysitting. Which he had thought was crazy—Ward Talley could have, and would have, paid her tuition. But Kathy was adamant about her independence. And all those causes. Marches, meetings, demonstrations. A creature of causes. And that was part of what drew Bernard to her, he *admired* her for her dedication to others. Her brand of fearlessness. About the only times he'd seen her show fear were about the children. Except for, damn it, whatever had gone down in Rincón Bay a year or two before they met. She'd never told him much about it, but he'd sensed her fear.

Now he went to what he half-jokingly called his study, the part of their bedroom with a long oak table pushed against the windows, next to it a bookshelf piled with books, magazines, files. He probably wasn't going to get any work done on the book now, but he'd rather shuffle through his notes than keep on with a conversation that—he knew, and she knew—would only devolve. When Kathy was on one of her crusades . . .

But this one, Bernard had an uneasy feeling about.

CHAPTER 4

Kathy sat on the deck of the townhouse the next evening as the sun was slowly sinking spectacularly behind the mountains. She had a coffee and the *Arizona Daily Star*. The sunset was unwatched, the paper unread; the coffee grew cold as she simply sat, too tired to move. She'd done a lot today, she reminded herself, teaching the first session of the new class, Arte para Latinas, sponsored by FAU—Feminist Artists United—at a place called Lola's Cantina, a gathering spot for LGBTQIA+ Latinx women.

Things had not gotten off to a great start there. She'd arrived early, as had a student, and somehow, they'd gotten into a near-shouting match about Kathy's beloved Goya.

Eventually, Lucha Matahombre ("Man-killer" in English: surely they had changed their last name, Kathy thought) threw a paintbrush at the wall and stomped away. Francisco Goya was a *man*. Therefore, he was unworthy of consideration.

The manager, a woman called Nora who was a tall and feathery but tough person, came over and smoothed things over with Lucha and helped Kathy set up. As they did, Nora talked a little. "You know, Lucha is . . . they've had a lot of trouble in their life. The others will be easy to deal with."

Kathy nodded. "I didn't mean to offend them, but . . ." Her hands, she noticed, were trembling slightly. She took a few deep breaths. She had really prepped for this class, researching women artists from Mexico and Central America. But Nora was way ahead of her. The brightly painted walls were covered with art, paintings, weavings, masks, collages, all by women and nonbinary artists, mostly for sale. And before the class started, Nora put on some music, a glorious, powerful voice. Chavela Vargas, she told Kathy, the great *lencha*—lesbian—singer from the 1950s on.

Apart from Lucha—who, to Kathy's surprise, decided to stay, a glowering presence at the far end of the long table—the others who drifted in seemed friendly or at least polite. Kathy, focusing on content over technique, got them started on self-portraits. When she happened to look up from the busy table, there was Corina's housekeeper/caregiver, Imalia, at the bar, talking and laughing with Nora.

They locked eyes, equally amazed. Neither could have expected to see the other at a Latinx lesbian bar in South Tucson. Imalia backed away and started to leave, but Kathy went after her. Imalia needed to know that she was welcome there.

As she did so, she heard Bernard's voice in her head. "Do you have to be there for every wounded soul?"

Who's put in my path? Yes. I do, she thought defiantly.

As Imalia seemed to have only enough English to get by on a rudimentary level with Corina, Kathy addressed her in the serviceable Spanish she'd picked up dealing with immigrants over the years and which was probably why FAU had wanted her to teach the class. "*Hola, Imalia! Estoy dando clases de dibujo aquí gratis, quieres participar?*"

Imalia shook her head. "No, I do not come for the class in *dibujo*—what is that in English? Señora Kathy, please do not say to Señora Corina I am here." She looked down, her cheeks a flaming dusty rose against her brown complexion.

"Imalia! Your life is your business. *Lo que haces en tu vida es negocio tuyo.* I'm just here to teach the class. My lips are sealed." How to say that in Spanish? "*Mis labios están cerrados* . . . Oh! Who's with Corina then?"

"She is at the PT. I go to her in one hour."

"Okay. Well, I've got to get back to this class."

Imalia smiled her timid smile and went to the bar, where she was soon laughing with Nora again.

The class had started out slow. The budding artists were self-conscious, but eventually she got them going with their self-portraits—tubs full of pencils, pens, watercolors, and pastels to choose from—and they didn't want to stop. The pitchers of sangria Nora served didn't hurt.

Finally, it was time. Kathy helped clean up and stored their work in a cupboard before waving goodbye to Nora and Imalia. Clearly a couple.

It had been a good day, but Kathy was worn out. In the car, with the air blasting, she remembered she hadn't talked to Corina that day, so she called her to see how PT went. Corina picked up immediately and whispered that somebody was stealing her money. *How could you possibly think that?* Kathy had almost said. Corina didn't deal with purchases anymore.

No cash, no credit cards. She calmed her down and promised to stop by tomorrow.

Now she just sat. She had wrested a cappuccino from the fancy machine Bernard had given her last Christmas, but there it sat, untouched. Spread before her was the familiar setting of the Catalinas rising in the background, the most beautiful time in the desert, but she barely saw it.

Kathy suddenly remembered there was a Border Aid meeting that night. She really should go: all the BA meetings were important, dealing with the endless issues of the endless flow of people from Central America and Mexico and more and more far-flung parts of the world to Arizona.

And where was Bernard? Out running, probably. He would gladly run to the ends of the earth if there were ends, she thought.

She must have nodded off, because she found herself in a dream about her parents.

"Mom? Dad?" she called.

But they stood like statues, then turned and walked away.

Kathy woke up with a choked feeling. It was a dream that seemed unremarkable but also deeply unsettling. And frightening.

She was thirsty but didn't move. Now it was dark. Bernard should be back. Instead of calling him, she thought about her father. Ward, home from the office, smelling of something sharp and exotic, not exactly pleasant but *him*. Her father. Her stolid mystery of a father. On the rare nights he didn't go into his den and shut the door, he would fall asleep in his chair in the living room after dinner to the television, as the kids scrabbled around him. Smelling the dad perfume. She remembered another smell that came later when she was home from college, that wafted from the bathroom when Pete was taking a bath and smoking a j.

In college, she'd found what seemed to be the perfect escape from her family. As the oldest Talley girl, inspired by a trip the family had taken a few years before, she'd been the first to leave the suburbs of New York for the exotic desert landscape of Tucson. The winter weather was glorious, and as a freshman at the U of A in Tucson, she thrived (until the shock of the fierce heat come May), enjoying the out-of-the-closet life for young people away from home in 1985, the smorgasbord of racial, gender, sexual freedom. She had a brief fling with her roommate, who smashed plates and moved out after Kathy told her, confessed really, that it turned out she was really only into men. Then she got involved with a Mexican American political organizer who turned out to be a shit, one of several. But she stayed at U of A until she graduated.

For grad school, though, she went back East, to NYU. Meeting Bernard at a multiethnic, multi-arts event in Washington Square Park was almost too good to be true. She thought he was sexy as hell, and his deep knowledge about Black music, especially jazz, was fascinating to her. Her love of art, meanwhile, intrigued him. Black and white didn't enter into the equation; they accepted each other for who they were. Or so it seemed then.

When not in bed, they spent a lot of time at downtown clubs and cafés and galleries. She turned him on to her favorite artists—Alice Neel, Romare Bearden, Rufino Tamayo,

Francisco Goya—more like introduced him to art in general as Bernard had been all about literature and music up to that point. In turn, he got her out of the punk and garage band scene, exposing her to his beloved jazz. At first, she told him she felt like her head would explode when they went to lofts and lolled on cushions listening to shrieking and honking saxophones and grim-faced drummers. "The bass is the anchor, follow the bass," he advised, and to her surprise, it worked. But God, was she glad when they started going to more mainstream clubs.

Bernard was also the first lover who could argue her to checkmate, and, she suspected, she was the first woman who could do so with him. Everything was so right. They were all over each other in a time and especially a place, the Lower East Side, where race didn't matter anymore, or so it seemed. Except . . . some disdainful and angry glances directed at her, mostly from white men and a few from Black women. The only wrinkle was the occasional times Bernard would pull back and brood in silence. In time, she came to understand: he'd been followed closely by a white clerk at a department store or a cab wouldn't stop for him, or a drunk would yell the N-word.

At one of the monthly dinners with her parents in the city, upscale places with solid silverware and roasted meats, places she would never otherwise go to even if she could have afforded to, Kathy announced she had something to tell them. Ward and Julia looked up from their filet mignon and salmon with the wariness that having four children instills in parents. Though the girls, as they still called Kathy, Corina, and Becca, had given them only minor trouble compared to Pete.

"I'm seeing a wonderful man." Kathy blushed with anger at herself. Why couldn't she just say it? *I'm living with a wonderful Black man.* "Well, we're together."

"A wonderful man *we haven't met*," Julia said.

"Who we'd like to meet," her father added.

"And you will! How about next Saturday? Come by my place for dinner. Bernard's a great cook."

Bernard had thought it would be better to meet in a restaurant. Neutral ground. But Kathy held firm. She wanted them to take in the whole picture, in one fell swoop.

After the Talleys had come and gone the next Saturday night, leaving partially eaten plates of Bernard's seafood risotto, Kathy and Bernard had their first real argument. Why hadn't she told them? Told them what? I told them you were wonderful, that's all they needed to know. Kathy, you saw their faces. You did! Like a rock had hit them on the head. When? When you opened the door, and there I was. A Black man. Bernard, this is 1992, that's over with. Done. Nah, it's not *over*, Kathy. You think it's over? It's never over. He left and got drunk at Bradley's, a jazz bar in the Village.

Yet they had survived for three-plus decades together. And Ward and Julia came around. They loved their grandchildren, and they grew to love Bernard too. Or at least like him. Bernard's dad, who everyone called Senior, was harder to read. But then, Bernard said, Senior was always hard to read. Bernard never said much about his family to Kathy. She fell into the stereotype of supposing he had a difficult upbringing in a struggling single-parent household, albeit one headed by the dad. Over time, she put together the pieces, a rather lonely-sounding childhood on the first floor of a two-story house in West Orange, New Jersey. Senior, Bernard Barris Senior, was a mechanical engineer who worked for forty years as a mechanical draftsman for Essex County in New Jersey. "Solid security and a pension," Senior had liked to say. What he didn't say was that the better-paying engineering jobs in the county almost always went to white men. As a kid, Bernard took piano lessons, although what he wanted to do was play basketball. They rarely saw relatives, who Senior called, simply, trouble. Kathy assumed his mother must have died, maybe in childbirth. In time, quite a long time, she learned that Louise Barris had announced she was a lesbian when he was an infant and split for Florida. But we communicate now, Bernard added. She's living her life and I'm fine with that.

Bernard was happy to go to City Hall to get married two years after they met but balked about a get-together afterward with his dad and her folks. "You've met my dad. You know he isn't into socializing."

"This is different. We're getting *married*."

"We've got that party with our friends."

"Our parents should meet."

Bernard caved. They got their license and celebrated at a Chinese restaurant nearby. The next day, they took the train from their apartment on the *Upper* Upper West Side, then a sketchy neighborhood just starting to gentrify, where you could still find affordable apartments, to the Talleys' white colonial in Westchester County. At the beautifully laid dining table, Ward and Bernard Barris Senior carried on in a brittle way that made Kathy want to scream and shake them both. Naturally, they talked about work. Ward asked about mechanical draftsmanship. "I'm a trained engineer, not a draftsman,"

Senior responded rather abruptly. In the silence that followed, Julia urged more prime rib on him. "Oh well, I'm just a slogan slinger," Ward said heartily then. Which was not true: he was an advertising executive who made a very decent living, having climbed the ladder the way every American was supposed to be able to do. Senior nodded and helped himself to the prime rib. Julia, who believed above all things in manners, said brightly, "Your work sounds fascinating but mysterious," before reaching for her wine glass and draining it. "Well!" she said and stood up, erect as a soldier. "I think it's time for the cake!" It was a splendid cake from that great French bakery in Mount Kisco.

"Well, now they've met, satisfied?" Bernard said later, after they'd finished the last of the champagne and Ward and Senior both handed them checks. Ward had driven what he called "the newlyweds" and Senior to the station. They stood on the platform, logy with food and drink and the strained atmosphere at the house. They heard the train approaching.

Senior enfolded Kathy in a quick hug. "Take care of this boy of mine." He tapped Bernard on the shoulder. "I'll let you two have your privacy." He gestured for them to enter the car in front of them, then walked down the platform to board the next one.

The moment he was out of earshot, Kathy sighed. "Maybe we should have just gone to the Village to hear some jazz like we were thinking..."

Bernard exhaled loudly. "*We* were thinking?" He checked his watch. "Hey, we still have time for the last set."

"I just want to go home," she said.

CHAPTER 5

Since the divorce three years before, Corina had stayed in the house. Tom had been generous about that—of course, he could afford to be, but still. It was a large house, with two living rooms, five bedrooms, a Viking kitchen, landscaped grounds, turquoise pool, expensive art they'd collected on their travels. (Tom lived in the beach house on Catalina now and had, to her surprise, taken little with him.) Every surface was cluttered, with files, stacks of papers, CDs, clothing, jewelry, which Corina would not allow anyone to touch, even though she never entertained or listened to music or wore the fancy clothes anymore. She wasn't allowed to cook anymore either—accidents with a knife, burners left on all night. These days, she lived on her beloved sushi and takeout Chinese food and no longer swam in the pool or drove her Mercedes SUV.

But Corina still had her enthusiasm for nature. She was constantly scouting for life from the patio, the birds drawn to the feeders, the rabbits, occasional snakes, and, above all, Henrique. When she'd spotted the tortoise after a long hiatus near that fence meant to keep out coyotes, she greeted him like he was the prodigal son. She'd been so certain she'd never see him again.

When it was too hot even to sit on the shaded patio with the fans blowing, she stayed in her bedroom or the little den off the kitchen. Imalia would put something on the television, and Corina would leaf through her boxes of loose photos from the pre-digital era, curling mounds of snapshots of her children, Tom, family, friends. Sometimes these trips down memory lane agitated her, even made her frenetic. This was exhausting for both her and Imalia, who watched her constantly, as if she were a toddler.

How she had fought the diagnosis! A blizzard of consults, trips to specialists out of state, meds, therapy, exercise, games to stimulate memory, and so on. But nothing stopped the scorched-earth march of her disease. Her world was cracked and slippery, thin ice through which she feared she would plunge into raging waters and be swept away. "My mind," she'd told Kathy recently in one of her lucid spells, "is going to become extinct." They'd hugged and cried. They had been so close once; now Alzheimer's had brought them close again.

Corina was terrified by what was happening to her, and it was still not very advanced. She was prey to sudden fits of claustrophobia that compelled her to try to escape. They had been warned about this. Doors outside were to be kept locked, keys hidden. But there were lapses. One morning, after a UPS man made a delivery and Imalia forgot to lock the front door after him, Corina slipped out and ran like a deer down the trail-like roads of the estate in the foothills. Imalia found her half an hour later, crouched behind a bush at Tessa and Tim's old elementary school.

She only knew this story because Kathy had told it to her later when she was trying to explain to Corina why she was no longer allowed the keys to her own house.

Corina had volunteered on committees at her kids' schools. Went to all the games, plays, presentations. On Halloween, when there was a parade from the school to the little park nearby, her kids' costumes, which they dreamed up and she fabricated, always won prizes; Tim as a washing machine took a first one year. Remembering these bits of her children's childhood, she sobbed happily. They were still wonderful children, just far away, grown up, not able to come be with her as often as she wished, which was every day.

Corina had been a fussy baby, a sensitive toddler. Kathy's little acolyte, her student, actor, illustrator, gofer, until, each time, her older sister pushed the envelope too hard, and Corina rebelled with a meltdown of tears. She asserted her independence by going to the University of Arizona in Tucson for college and, after graduation, staying there instead of going back East as Julia and Ward had hoped, even expected.

In the mid-1990s, Kathy and Bernard, recently married, moved to Tucson for Bernard's doctorate and were renting a little house. Corina had a small apartment nearby and managed on her social worker salary. She dated but nothing stuck. Then she met Tom Swanson at a popular bar on the East side. Tom was good-looking, charming; he liked nature as much as she did and he liked living well, above his means perhaps, but Corina discovered she liked it too—the expensive restaurants, the exciting trips. He was a natural-born dealmaker, a professional optimist with a hearty, distinctive laugh that, looking back when the marriage was falling apart, Corina thought might be as much the secret of his success as anything else: his con man's laugh, which made you feel that life was a grand thing.

Within a year, they were living together. Three years later, they moved from their nice townhouse into a fancier one, and from there to the house, on two lots in the most desirable part of town. Corina quit her job, focused on the remodeling and the landscaping and the decorating. They traveled a lot. Fly-fishing in Colorado one week, swimming in Cabo the next, Europe in the fall, Southeast Asia in the winter. And they entertained when they were in town. Fancy soirees once Tom joined the boards of the art museum, a youth-at-risk program, the botanical garden. They acquired the beach house in California, a "cabin" in Aspen (houses in Marrakesh and Havana came later). Corina's hair and clothes were LA-red-carpet ready. Their two children, Tessa and Tim, a girl and a boy, completed the picture. Then Tom bought a restaurant, made it fancy nouveau Mexican, called it "Tomás," and was there almost every night when he was in town. He claimed he did a lot of business there. But Corina knew he was partying hard.

To Kathy, Becca, and their spouses, Corina and Tom's life was like some Hollywood movie, and they were not Hollywood-movie types. They never pretended to enjoy the dress-up dinner parties Corina and Tom threw at their lavish home for Tucson's surprisingly robust cohort of beautiful people, a lot of them refugees from California, and gradually, they'd stopped going. The sisters still got together but not as often. Neither Becca nor Kathy ever said as much, but Corina knew they thought she had become something of a stranger. A poseur, even. Always shopping, entertaining, traveling.

Then Tessa and Tim left for college and Corina had too much time on her hands. Time to think. Of course, there was the garden, cooking, shopping, traveling, but Tom often traveled without her now, to his properties in the Southwest and with his new (very rich) partner, Tomás. (Of course, they made a joke of it, the Tom and Tomás show. The show involved a lot of cocaine, Corina suspected.) Corina realized she was tired of her arm-candy role. She found a highly recommended therapist, who diagnosed anxiety and depression. Meds helped at first and then not so much.

One afternoon, when Kathy suggested she might do some volunteering again, Corina burst into tears. "You don't get it," she said. "I'm not myself." Something was wrong with her shoulder, she added, probably a pinched nerve. And she had digestive problems. And she couldn't sleep without taking Ambien anymore.

She started forgetting words then, added flour instead of sugar to recipes, couldn't find even simple things like her toothpaste in its glass. Her internist referred her to a psychiatrist, Dr. Lorber. She ordered a flurry of tests—neurological, blood, CT scan, MRI, EEG, all inconclusive.

It was difficult to map the glacial, subtle changes of early dementia and too soon, Dr. Lorber thought, for the expensive PET test that measured for the proteins thought to be associated with cognitive dementia. But she put Corina on AChE inhibitors in any case, along with the antidepressant and antianxiety meds that kept needing to be tweaked.

As far as anyone could tell, nothing she took was helping any.

CHAPTER 6

Everybody called Toby Radner "Toby" except his father, who insisted on Tobias, the name on his birth certificate. "Tobias" was in homage of Len Radner's favorite player on his college basketball team, Tobias Jorgensen (center forward). To Len's deep, if mostly unspoken, disappointment, his son had never thrived on the basketball court as he had done. Toby had always preferred books and music.

Toby reached into the chipped but still beautiful bowl Becca had insisted on buying, though it was over their budget, on that trip to Greece. She kept it filled with fruits in season, peaches now. He felt around the peaches slowly, cautiously—a habit that he knew drove Becca crazy, when she was there to witness it. A decisive woman, when she wanted some fruit, she simply reached into the bowl and grabbed a piece. Toby, in contrast, dithered. He liked to take his time to palm them, sometimes stopping for long moments as something extraneous struck him. As now, when the Greek bowl transported him back to the Greek isles. A short mental hop to years later, when they introduced young Cam to the beauties of Greece, and how their son had been at his most peaceful in a short but already turbulent life while they were there.

Toby sighed and returned to the business of choosing a peach, fingering them, looking out for those bruise spots that turned so quickly into pockets of brown slush. Finally, he made his choice, lifted it out of the bowl and up to his mouth.

He bit in gingerly, thinking as he did so that eating a peach almost felt like tearing into human flesh. His heart was torn, he thought, bit after bit of it smashed. Like the holes he'd discovered Cam had smashed in the walls of his room during some rage attack . . . and now rage surged into *him*. How dare his son smash his walls, smash the hopes he and Becca had for him?

He put his half-eaten piece of fruit down with, yes, a flare of anger.

Not sweet enough. You could never tell with peaches.

The doorbell that was rarely used rang. Toby discarded the remains of the fruit in the trash and went to the door, on the other side of which Phil, handyman and friend, stood smiling with a toolbox. The plan was that Cam was supposed to help Phil fix his wall—the gaping holes—but when Toby had gone looking for him five minutes ago, he'd discovered the boy had snuck out of the house already. Becca was going to lose it when she found out.

"Hey," Phil said.

"Hey." Toby motioned him inside, wondering, *When did "hi" turn into "hey" for people their age?* "It's you and me, pal, the kid stepped out."

Phil set down the toolbox. "Done a runner, hey?" He fist-bumped. "On it, bro."

Toby led him upstairs, rolling his eyes a little. *"Hey"? "Bro"? Teenage fist bump?* The *dude* was what, close to sixty? But, *hey,* Phil was a nice guy and out of work, hence this wall-repair gig.

Toby opened the door to Cam's room. "This is it," he said unnecessarily.

"Whoa, yeah, he did a number here." Maybe sensing Toby's darkening mood, Phil stopped talking, segueing into professional mode with his gear.

"Coffee?" Toby offered.

At Phil's eager nod, he went to get him a coffee and bring the buckets of spackle and paint up after. At least Cam could do the paint job.

When Toby handed him his double espresso, Phil assured him he could handle the whole wall repair by himself. "Easy-peasy. I know you got a bunch of deadlines," he added.

Toby nodded mendaciously, pretending to agree, and split to his office downstairs, where he sat looking at his blank computer screen and sipped his own double espresso. Deadlines? Not exactly. Stuff on spec, proposal after proposal falling into the black hole of unanswered emails, phone calls. Apparently, he was dead to "the industry," gold turned to shit. It was the timing, man. That's what everybody said. *Whatever happened to rock and roll will never die?*

The thing was that Toby focused on the outliers, really good ones, but nobody under thirty seemed to have heard of them or cared if they had. *Okay, Elvis, Otis, but what about the Stone Poneys?* He sighed and started typing. Maybe he'd hear back from somebody today.

"Hello!" Becca stood outside the office, overflowing grocery bags in hand.

How much time had gone by? "You went shopping?" he said incredulously. Shopping was *his* gig. He, for example, would not have gotten those peaches. Also, grocery shopping got him away from the black hole that seemed to be his profession lately. Lately, as in the past six, seven years.

"These are heavy."

Toby stepped forward and took two bags from Becca. "I was gonna do it later."

"Well, now you won't have to."

He followed her back into the odd-shaped kitchen, which was homey, thanks to Becca, despite its inescapable carved-out-of-a-closet look. "I know Whole Foods is your happy place," she said, "but sometimes I need one too."

She was in a mood, understandably.

"Phil's still here," he said.

Bags went on the counter. "And Cam is helping him?"

He began unloading a bag, examining each item. "Uh, he's ... Oh, did you buy more rice? We've already got jasmine, basmati, arborio. What's this 'bomba' stuff?" he asked, holding up the packet she'd bought.

"A guy at the store said it's the best rice for paella."

"Are we making paella? Ambitious."

"Stop talking about the frigging rice! *Is Cam helping Phil?*"

Toby set down the bomba as carefully as if, he thought, it were an actual bomb that might go off. "No."

"Are you fucking kidding me? Did he sneak out again?"

"Apparently."

"Apparently? Toby, you were supposed to make sure he stayed and fixed the wall of our house that we are graciously allowing him to live in. That he trashed."

"He's gonna do the painting," Toby said feebly. "I'll make sure."

"Oh? How? Lock him in with a brush? That'll work. He'll probably smear it all over the floor. We've got to do something and *you know it*."

Now she was pacing.

"Is there anything that needs to go in the freezer? Ice cream? Mint chocolate chip, I hope? B&J?"

She produced a container of his favorite ice cream, tossed it to him—or, more accurately, at him. Then she slid to the floor in tears.

Naturally, Phil chose that moment to walk in, hands and work pants already splattered with spackle. Becca looked up sharply and began to howl, softly, into her cupped hands.

"Mm, sorry," Phil said. "Tough time for you guys. Uh, Toby, need you to turn the power off. Just for a few minutes."

Since Phil, Becca, and Toby all belonged to 12-step groups (Phil in AA, Toby in Debtors Anonymous, Becca in Al-Anon) where sharing painful truths was routine, Phil's appearance during Becca's meltdown wasn't as embarrassing as it might have been.

"Anything I can do?" he added, half crouching before Becca.

She didn't look up. Toby leaned against the counter with one hand shielding his eyes.

"Well, we can circle back later," Phil said.

For some reason, Becca reacted strongly to the seemingly innocuous statement.

"Circle back! I'm done circling!" she said. She was forty-five, still as limber as a twenty-something, and a force of nature. She claimed it was because she was the youngest child and had a brother two years older who had constantly picked on her. She leapt to her feet, opened a closet, and clicked a breaker. Though it was a sunny day, everything went dim inside with the loss of power.

"Shit, you could have waited till I saved my file!" Toby said in a higher voice than usual. If he lost all that work because of her tantrum...

"It automatically saves, Toby," she yelled as he charged off.

She followed him to the office—she always called it his "lair"—and there they picked up the argument they'd been having for the better part of a year.

Becca: "So what are we going to do? Therapy isn't helping. He ignores our rules."

Toby: "He promised me last night he'll do that anger-management class."

Becca: "Good, but I want to take away his bong. I want to smash it with a hammer."

Toby: "Good luck with that. You know he'll just get another one."

Becca: "Do you even hear us? We're hostages, Toby. We've got to set more boundaries and stick to them."

Toby: "Or what? I don't want to lose him. We'll lose him, Becca."

Becca. "He smashed up his room and he's out getting high somewhere. We have to do something. That camp place the Havers sent their kid worked wonders."

Silence.

"You can turn the power back on!" Phil shouted down.

Becca wiped her eyes and went to the kitchen to flick the breaker back on. Power restored, Toby rebooted his computer and was relieved to see that, as inscrutable and at times unreliable as it could be, it had, as Becca claimed it would, autosaved the pitch piece he'd been working on for two days. *Piece of bullshit*, he thought in down moments, though when he was up it was his *incisive elevator pitch*, as when a movie producer is stuck in an elevator with you and in one minute or less, you've got to convince him to buy your show. For now, he had nothing, neither bullshit nor insight to add to it. He picked up his guitar. John Prine time.

Hearing Toby's plangent, melancholy plucking flicked the anger switch on again in Becca. She slammed the chicken breasts she'd removed from the freezer down on the counter. She told the wall, "I need to get out of here!"

She went to her study, another little room that had been a closet when they moved into the house twelve years ago. Everything was in its place, the Buddhas tucked in the corners, the books neat on the shelves, the little desk that she only used for bill-paying and such. She picked up one of the manila folders with her poetry that had been rarely opened until recently. She sat cross-legged on the floor, took out a yellow pad from the folder and a pen.

> *The silver-gray of the web*
> *Spun in the corner of the window,*
> *glinting when I pull up the blinds.*
> *Burnt-brown stick arms and legs,*

An insect trussed and dead not dying,
I hope. Though I am not overly concerned with the prey.
It is the spider, a nightmare presence,
spring-loaded clump of arachnid legs
foreshadowing something's violent end.
The captive twists in the web,
Awaiting its consumption.
This may be the billionth time. Ten billionth. Ten times ten billionth.
Hard to believe in a god that leaves his creatures to their own devices
to find a way out of the nightmare end.
I will need to use my teeth here.

She stopped writing. She was too tired to cry; her body was washed out with flu-like symptoms she supposed were from shock. Cam, Cameron Charles, tearing at her insides as he had done when he was born, a wild puppy. And she a fierce and tender guard dog. Perhaps it was a rite of passage, hell yes it was, to shred in his half-manhood the mother who had and would give anything for her child, only to find how much this devotion was resented. She had loved him always, at first the idea of him and then the solid physicality, the blast and jolts of his flesh coming from hers with lavish disregard. And she did not understand another way to do so. Yes, she went to Al-Anon, but that was because of Dad and Pete. Cam was her *son*. There could be no such thing as the so-called healthy distancing that the seasoned veterans she met at those meetings espoused. And her sisters had no idea; their kids had got into trouble, sure, but just the usual teenage wacked-brain stuff. Older now, they all seemed to be sailing smoothly into adulthood. But her boy Cam was a whirling dervish of boundless ADHD energy unleashed on her nerves. Dervishes do not make team players; on the courts and fields of preening boyhood, he'd been snickered at and jeered at and had fights or, worse, was ignored. Becca had stepped up, signed him up for boxing lessons, guitar lessons... Cam must be saved. Who else could do it? Recently, she'd learned, he'd become the boy who supplied the team players their fake IDs, their booze, and maybe even their drugs.

Becca's vigilance, and, in his less focused way, Toby's, meant next to nothing to Cam. For every vodka bottle or pill bottle or stash of weed they confiscated, there were bushes, basements, other kids' houses, an arsenal of bongs and baggies and bottles. She understood that they had been ground down into a holding pattern that was, really, submission to his will. She wanted him to get help. She wanted him to go away!

Becca shoved her hatchling poem into the folder and sat at her desk. She must attend to the business of Cam's latest trouble now. Toby wavered, dallied, grew despondent when negative communiqués arrived from the authorities. Had been arriving more frequently. It was she who dealt with the gatekeepers of a teenaged boy's life.

To the parents of Cameron Radner:
It has come to our attention that...
We regret to inform you that...

She had researched and found: child psychologists, adolescent psychiatrists, school aides, tutors, doctors, dentists, summer camps, enrichment activities, and now, to Toby's distress (what about her?!), she was on to rehabs. As it was down to her to hold down a job to pay the majority of the bills. When all she wanted to do, if she were honest, was be in this cool, quiet room and write her poetry. For God's sake, how many poems had been aborted in all her efforts for Cam? If it weren't for him, would she be leading the life of a poet?

If she could even dare to call herself a poet.

CHAPTER 7

Kathy flopped down on the couch. Being out in the heat usually made her want to take a nap.

Before she knew it, she was waking up. A vigorous dreamer, Kathy often cadged ideas for painting from the fragments that hovered when she awoke. But today she had a sense of apprehension, though it took a few moments for her to connect the feeling to the upcoming trip to Rincón Bay. Yet she was aware of another feeling too—a kind of impatience to see the place.

She fed the yowling cat, Balloon, and made coffee, then checked her phone, which she had put on silent and neglected. There was a cascade of messages from Border Aid. But she decided that for once, she'd stay home and work on her own art: the *Discordia* collages and paintings. Eris was the Greek equivalent of Discordia, only a letter away from Eros. An ancient Hellenic joke? She needed to get going; the deadline for the show was six weeks away. She went to her tiny studio.

When her phone, restored from limbo, buzzed, Kathy ignored it. Five minutes later, it buzzed again. Then again. She gave up. Were all the members of Border Aid stalking her? But it was Pete.

"Hey," she said, trying to keep the worry out of her voice.

"I don't know about this trip to the beach," Pete said with no preliminaries. "It's a long drive and I can't eat Mexican food anymore."

Part of her wanted to say, *Fine, don't come, you're a pain in the ass anyway,* but she ignored that part and instead calmed him down. He could sleep in the car, there was other cuisine there (pizza, fish), he loved the beach, the doctor had said okay.

They ended the call just as she heard Bernard come in.

"Hey, you're home? I thought you had a meeting or a class."

"I decided to work. I have that show coming up." When he didn't react or move from the doorway of her glorified closet, she added, "Something wrong?"

"No. Yeah. Matterson. He's after me to teach another class next semester. Wasn't happy when I said no." Leo Matterson was the new head of the music department. The job Bernard thought he'd get.

"He's such a weasel."

"Are weasels lazy?" Bernard wondered. "'Cause that dude is always trying to palm stuff off."

"But you said no? I wish I could do that more often."

"Yeah, well, you know how I feel about that."

"I'm home, aren't I?"

"Yeah. Bravo. Calls for a drink."

She put down the brush she had just picked up, sighed, and followed him to the kitchen, where he got two Coronas out of the fridge. They clinked bottles.

"To your skipping a meeting."

"To your not working on the book." She wondered idly if she would be saying those words for another five years. Maybe forever.

After the beer, Bernard went to his desk in the bedroom and Kathy went back to her studio. But instead of working on her current drawing, a Goyaesque tableau of people on their knees in the desert raising their arms for bottles of water that hovered just beyond their reach, she sat unseeing, feeling unsettled by her husband's generalized anger and resentment.

"You and I are codependents, like Mom," Becca had told her, more than once. Her theory was that their parents had seen the world through either side of a martini glass. "But 'codependents' is one of those fuzzy words," Kathy had protested. Still, she thought Becca was at least partly right. You didn't have to be in Al-Anon to recognize there was a shitload of psychic residue involved in dealing with an alcoholic parent while the other parent was pretending that everything was fine, and exhausting themselves with the effort. So that Kathy, Becca—all of them—grew up with a model of a charade, a baseline uncertainty about what was real, with no way as children to articulate it, only to feel the effects of a heavily redacted truth and emotional unavailability. There was so much stress trying to negotiate a childhood where they were told that everything was fine but they knew it was not, and so they imagined what lay behind the facade (worse than the suppressed reality). It carved out ruts in their brains fueled by stress's gift of cortisol as they grew up. As the eldest sibling (Becca's explanation went on), Kathy was the shock troop, chosen by birth order to try to negotiate the childhood landscape. Had she developed a kind of hypervigilance as a result?

"Look, I know you tried to help us even while you were rebelling," Becca went on. "We all craved their attention, though by the time they had me, Ward and Julia were more, oh, what's the word I want?—adept?—at handling kids. But of course, on the other hand, Pete just wore them out. So maybe that's why they were at least more mellow with me."

Thanks to Dr. Anne Maples (the ostensible catalyst for going to therapy had been Kathy's son Theo's gayness, or rather, his constant change of partners), Kathy felt she had mostly come to terms with her perhaps outsized role as rescuer. Yes, her mother had been one to the max—shielding her husband and then her son from reality's consequences. But Kathy resisted finding a parallel to her own actions. In fact, it infuriated her to even think so.

"Yet to you," Anne had once said, her lips slightly upturned, "isn't there something familiar about seeing danger around the corner and feeling that you have to rush in and fix it? Does it seem logical to you, growing up with a father who was an alcoholic and a Sisyphean mother cleaning up, hiding, reinventing?"

"Well, look at the world!" Kathy had shouted at placid Anne. "I can't ignore people who are suffering *from no fault of their own*. I've got to do something about it!"

"From no fault of their own," Anne repeated softly and gave her what Kathy thought of as "the look."

This conversation had gone down not long after she'd been introduced to Border Aid, one of several organizations that ministered to people trying to get to the promised land on the other side of Mexico.

"So many die and are never found. Children!" she sputtered. "They have nothing!

"Yes, it's admirable, wonderful," Ann agreed. "There's disaster and there's help, healing. You jump in and help. But is there also a lack of balance here? You have shared your concerns about not being home as much as you would like for your own family. And for your art. Yourself."

So many times, during the years of juggling work and raising a family, it was Bernard who came home after a day of teaching and made dinner and supervised the kids' homework and got them ready for bed. Because Kathy had meetings. When the kids were older, they got on her case about it, complained she was preoccupied with her own stuff. How could *she* tell them what to do?

Even now, in their twenties, flown from the nest, this dynamic persisted. Tamara had recently come back during a college break, sleeping in the tiny spare room in the downsized condo. She was between boyfriends again. She claimed she wasn't particularly bothered about it, although she'd lyricized about a Rodrigo, or was it Roberto, only a month before on the phone.

One evening during her visit, Tamara borrowed the car to meet some guy she'd met on a dating site. Kathy went to bed at eleven. Bernard, who always got up early for a run, was already asleep, snoring lightly. By midnight, Kathy's NP (as she called negative projection, another term Becca had taught her) was efficiently working up disaster scenarios: Tamara lying unconscious by the side of a road, Tamara brutally attacked by the internet date. She called her daughter three times, but it went straight to voicemail.

Suddenly, she had to get up, do something.

Kathy was cleaning out the refrigerator when Tamara came in the house. Beautiful, unharmed.

"Mom? Why did you keep calling me? It's so annoying. *What are you doing?*"

"Nice to see you too." Kathy peeled off her rubber gloves. "Two rotten peaches, one onion reduced to slush, a bag of green beans turned to *fuzz.*"

"I said, 'What. Are. You. Doing. Waiting up for me.'" Tamara threw her bag at the counter. It missed and fell to the floor, contents spilling out—pack of condoms, bong, cigarettes. She bent and hurriedly scooped them up. "Mom, stop. You never change! I'm managing my life just fine! *I'm* going to bed now. Safe and sound, Mom."

"I just worry because I'm your mother. Did you have a good time?"

Tamara shot her a look. "Not really. Oh, *Mom.*" She gave her mother a brief hug and trudged down the hall to the spare bedroom.

The next day over breakfast, Tamara suggested that Kathy take up meditation. "Or tai chi. Something centering. You're either running all over tending to your lost sheep or you're freaking out about us."

Kathy felt like yelling at her, *But don't you remember? When I held you, sang to you, read to you? You were four when you thought the furniture came alive with monsters, five I think when you walked barefoot into a wasp nest, ten when you broke your ankle, thirteen when your best friend rejected you for that new girl. And I was there! I got Toni Morrison and Angela Davis on the reading list in high school. I went to the principal when kids teased you about your "bad" hair. I took you to that spa place when you had your heart broken by that Kaylong dude. I helped you with college-admissions stuff.*

As if she was reading her mother's mind, Tamara said, "Mom, I'm not guilting you. You've always tried to be there for me." She sighed. "Will you please think about letting up on all this stuff you do? That artists' collective, the immigrant things, the kids flunking out of community college. Let somebody else do it. Hang out with Dad."

"I'll think about it," Kathy said, stung.

Now, in her studio, Kathy wondered why, for the umpteenth time, since negative projection bears sterile fruit and makes a person anything from uncomfortable to panicked, she didn't ease up.

You can't, she thought. She cleaned her brushes and tidied up.

CHAPTER 8

Just two years apart, Corina and Kathy shared everything about each other growing up—until boys came into the picture. Kathy couldn't understand what she called Corina's "taste" in men and vice versa. In college, Kathy went for (in Corina's opinion) the obviously emotionally unavailable types, while Corina fell for (in Kathy's view) the bullies. Then Kathy met Bernard (it was unthinkable to call him Bernie, and so no one did)—single, gorgeous, smart, stable, employed.

Not long after, Corina met Tom Swanson.

One night Kathy and Bernard happened to be at Tina's, a bar favored by grad students and faculty at the U of A in Tucson and met the famous Tom. He insisted on paying for their drinks and invited them to a jazz concert the next weekend at an art gallery a friend of his ran. With his devilish grin, ready laugh, and openness, Tom made Bernard feel right at home. Kathy, not so much. Tom seemed too good to be true. A player. But Corina was enthralled and soon they were living together, and he was making more and more money doing real estate deals. They got married. They had children. He got rich. Richer.

The first bankruptcy came about ten years later. Corina avoided her sisters during the worst of that but, with expensive lawyers, Tom was soon back in the game. And he just got more and more successful, which meant more and more stuff, houses, art, cars, trips. And lots of business trips, golf weekends with clients at scenic resorts, LA, New York. For the kids, Tessa and Tim, their dad was more like an event; the everyday stuff was down to Corina. But she didn't complain. When he was home, it was all about good times, throwing parties, buying antiques and paintings, and an unending, in fact increasing, fondness for reminiscing about his hardscrabble past as a farm boy from Iowa (no indoor plumbing until he was a teenager), getting up before dawn to help feed the animals, milk the cows. He talked as if it were all a great joke.

Opportunities opened up in Cuba and Morocco, where he and his business partner, Tomás, visited often enough that it made sense to buy houses there. Though somehow, Corina never made it to Havana or Marrakech. Then came the second bankruptcy. This one was a lot tougher and locally notorious. The Swansons were put on a strict budget by the government; their expenses were scrutinized monthly, with little discretionary spending allowed. This crackdown went on for nearly three years, during which Tom was eased off the prestigious boards he served on, they stopped getting invited to fancy parties, and a lot of their friends evaporated.

During that awful period before the divorce, Kathy and her sister were on a hike one day when Corina had a meltdown: she had found out Tom was still cheating on her; in fact, he had girls installed in the houses in Havana and Marrakesh—and he didn't feel guilty about it.

Still? Kathy thought. *As in, he was cheating on you before? WTF? You've never even hinted about any of this before.* "You need to get a divorce," she told her, handing Corina yet another tissue as they sat cooling their feet in a stream.

Corina sobbed harder, shaking her head. "You don't understand."

When she called Kathy a few weeks later to invite her and Bernard to her house for Bernard's birthday as if nothing had happened, Kathy's first impulse was to say no. She wanted nothing more to do with Tom. But Corina begged her to come, so they did.

Tom was as smoothly ebullient as ever that night, but for Kathy, it had all worn as thin as his back hair. So what if he gave Bernard a painting, by someone he said was a well-known Moroccan artist, of Afro-Bedouins in colorful flowing robes, backgrounded by the mountains near the village of Merzouga? *He buys his way out of everything*, she thought.

Tom had showed Corina the painting a month before during one of his increasingly rare weeks at home—as she was pulling down the bedcovers of their vast Alaskan King bed, in which they still slept together in these interludes.

"Isn't it kind of... insulting, don't you think?" she asked him.

"What? Why?"

"Well, they could never afford a painting like that. For one thing."

"It's quality work!"

"Yes, but it's . . ." She struggled for the right words. "It's clearly expensive. Showing off. Always the big man. Like that Lamborghini you got, for heaven's sake."

Tom flung himself onto his side of the bed and picked up a magazine from the nightstand. He flipped through it as if engrossed. "I got a good deal on it."

Corina sat down on her side of the bed with a thump, her heart racing. She was surprised at how angry she was.

"Plus, Bernard's Black."

"So I've noticed. It's a painting of Black Arabs. Which I happen to think he'll find fascinating."

"I mean, white guy gives Black guy an expensive painting of Black guys? It could be seen as racially patronizing."

"Christ!" Tom hurled the magazine at a wall and jumped up. "What's the real problem here, Corina?"

Corina blew her nose and said, "You have never taken me to Morocco. Or Cuba either."

"Christ, not this again. Please. It's all business when I'm there."

"*Tell me.*"

"Tell you what?"

"What is her name?" She laughed shrilly. "Or do I mean *their* names?"

"I said it's business, Corina; it doesn't have anything to do with us." Tom pulled on his bathrobe and left, closing the door sharply.

Later, unable to sleep, Corina went to the cavernous room they'd added on during a remodel—Tom's man cave. Giant TV, pool table, and bar. He was asleep on the buttery, oversize leather couch, his mouth open, a line of drool trailing the expensive fabric. A football game was playing on the giant screen. She clicked it off and stood over him, looking at him as carefully as she'd seen Kathy look when she was painting.

In sleep, his cheeks sagged into nascent jowls and the dark shadow on his chin gave him a disreputable, even rascally look. Tom stirred and threw an arm out, as if in protest.

Corina turned and went back to their bedroom at the other end of the house, lay back down in their enormous bed. She didn't sleep.

Early in the morning, she went to the kitchen and made the coffee as Tom liked it, extra-dark and extra-strong. She took a cup, black, two sugars, to the man cave and set it down and said his name, over and over, until he surfaced.

"What, what?" he said, sitting up and blearily taking the cup. "Thanks. But Jesus, what time is it?"

"Six thirty. By the way, I'm calling Caitlin Morrisey this morning."

Hot coffee splashed on his arm as he sat straight up. "Caitlin Morrisey!"

She was part of their circle, though not a friend. Had been on the board of the art museum with Tom. She was a high-powered divorce lawyer.

"Corina," he said. "You won't do it. You like our life too much. And I'm here, aren't I?" He tried to pull her down to him.

She slapped him.

CHAPTER 9

Half a container of Boost, that was all Pete could get down today. He could hear the nurse nagging him when she weighed him in tomorrow before dialysis: "Pete, Pete, are you eating those small meals five times a day like we said? Drinking your shakes?"

Yada yada yada, he knew the drill. He looked down at the bulge extending from his middle. Like he was ready to give birth. Meanwhile, he was skinnier than he'd ever been in his life. Go figure.

Half a container, best he could do.

Pete slid into the ancient Barcalounger (it had been Ward Talley's as the couch had been Julia's favorite seat) and clicked on the remote. At least he had cable. No internet right now, long story. His sisters had gotten him two laptops—was it his fault they'd been attacked by viruses? He didn't need any lectures from them, and anyway, what was a laptop or *ten* laptops to Corina? Okay, she paid most of his rent, the bills, threw in a few hundred a month for what she called "discretionary spending." He was supposed to be eternally grateful? Fuck that; he was a sick man.

He clicked on TCM and, as usual, slid into the haze of the past, another cheesy black-and-white movie. He roused for a moment and thought maybe he'd switch to ESPN. But the games really put him to sleep now. He'd rather try to stay awake and watch Robert Mitchum snarl. He felt both heavy and light, pinned down to the Barcalounger but with his head seeming to be hovering around the ceiling, silvered and crumpled memories flipping by, like the actual photos that people used to take. That his dad had taken, including dozens of Pete. Pitching for West Farms High. Only for a year, but what a year. He'd ended up with a seventy-five-miles-per-hour average, pretty amazing for a junior. Who knows, maybe he would have gone on to the minors. At the least. But then came juvie hall.

It was all down to Thor, the old dope-smoking schemer. Who the hell is called Thor anyway? But before the backlash when they got caught, they'd had some good times. That cruise to Jamaica? Rastas, man! Awesome parties. He and Thor rented a boat and took a few of the fellas out, who'd provided the ganja. Pretty awesome for two seventeen-year-olds! Almost made up for what came later back at home. They'd been slick, nabbing houses in the hood when no one was home, gloves on, quiet as mice as they boosted TVs, jewelry, a couple of fur coats. Driving into Harlem to Thor's fence. Until that last time. At least they let Pete play ball at juvie.

Then when he got out, Thor said, this fucking town, let's go to LA. So Pete snuck out in the middle of the night, threw his duffel into Thor's Pinto, and off they went. He remembered when they were in Pennsylvania that he'd forgotten to leave a note for his parents. Too late.

What a piece of junk that Pinto was, but the beater made it somehow all the way to Venice, California. Where Pete planned to learn how to surf, maybe get a landscaping job. Legit stuff. But it appeared that everybody else out there had the same idea. Luckily, he scored a wallet off a drunk in some dive bar. Dude must have just gotten paid or something, 'cause there was 450 dollars in it.

Thor left before the band hit that night—took off with some skinny girl who smiled like her lips were glued together, to hide what was left of her speed-freak teeth, probably—but Pete stayed and didn't even drink much once the band that had been lurking in a corner started playing.

Crowguts, it was called, black paint across an American flag on the wall. At first, Pete was perplexed by the sounds those dudes were making. He didn't know whether to throw his empty Coors bottles at them or get down on his knees and genuflect. A bunch of hippies walked out. Then he knew he dug the stuff. It was some crazy forward-looking stuff. Somebody said it was called "grunge."

Thor fucked up soon after. They had to get out of town, took a Greyhound to Chicago where Thor had a cousin with a crash pad with no heat and, dude, this was Chicago in late November. But it was free. Thor started moving some product, but Pete didn't want to get involved and he hated what he saw of Chicago, which was not much, but the cold was like the Arctic Circle and he got mugged one night. At least he didn't get shot, Thor helpfully pointed out. But Pete had had it by then. He called the parents, who wired him money for another Greyhound back to the Northeast.

When he got back, he scored a job working part-time at a hardware store in Mount Kisco and thought he'd check out the community college. Not in a million years did he plan on breaking into Cindy Porter's house—that was all down to a bad acid trip—and he didn't *do* anything to her. Was just standing there when she woke up and started screaming. Why did they have to call the cops?

Ward bailed him out, not exactly 100 percent sober himself judging from the familiar aroma emanating from him. Didn't say a word, hunched over the steering wheel driving home. But Julia had a fine speech for him, tears running down her face, guilting him up, down, and sideways. Shocked him in the end, told him he had to leave, he could go stay at a Y in Manhattan. He packed his duffel and the next morning Ward again drove him, but this time he actually spoke to him. "Five hundred dollars, son. Spend it wisely and get yourself a steady job because this is the end of it." Then to Pete's horror, his dad's face crumpled up and he made choking sounds. Pete quickly got out of the car to wait for the train to the city. This was not a good memory.

Finally, a stroke of luck when Ward and Julia decided to retire a year later and move to Tucson—all the girls were there by then—and took Pete with them. He golfed with Ward at the club and got a kick out of it, all those old Republican duffers. He took a six-week course in air-conditioning maintenance and got a part-time job. Man, he was straight then, the odd six-pack was all. He felt good for the first time in years. Then his new buddy from work, Brad, told him about the trailer park—cheap, lots of parties. Pete got Julia to convince Ward they should buy him a trailer.

So then that turned to shit, a little too deep into the substances, especially after he hurt his back on the job. Workers' comp was nice, sure, but there were some rough times, to put it mildly.

But look at him now. Nice apartment, car, no hanky-panky. The little studio where he could jam to his heart's content. Okay, his kidneys and his heart were problematic and he got tired pretty fast. But still. He was kickin' it.

Head back and mouth open in the Barcalounger, Pete hovered between memories, sleep, and watching Robert Mitchum. God, he missed having friends around though. This apartment complex was full of young families or old folks. Nobody to hang with. He wondered if—no, he *knew*—that this was his fate, loneliness like a heavy blanket glued to his back. But as soon as he was done resting, he'd go jam.

Once, decades ago now, Pete went with Kathy and Bernard to some jazz loft in Alphabet City in Manhattan. Bernard warned him the music was avant-garde, so expect anything. He kinda loved it, but his thing (as they knew) was Captain Beefheart. Ever since he heard the Crowguts do what he later learned was *Trout Mask Replica*. A hair-raising, mesmerizing great mess of sound. From the Beefster he got into the Mothers of Invention and Soft Machine and Van der Graaf Generator, music from a bygone decade, but he belonged to it for eternity. "So it goes, so it goes," he murmured, now more or less awake. "I coulda been a contender," he added in what he thought of as a Brooklyn accent.

Somebody was knocking at the door. Pete groaned and got up. Kathy again! One of Grandma Talley's homely sayings popped in his mind: "like a bad penny."

"What?" he said, opening the door.

"You're in a mood." She moved to the living room, three steps, and swept some crumbs from the couch before sitting down.

"You too."

She stopped frowning, pulled some paperwork out of her bag, and waved it at him.

Always something, he thought.

"Your living will has to be notarized. Pete, don't groan, it's the last document we need."

"Thank God."

"Have you even looked at it?"

No, he hadn't looked at it. He took it from her, swept down the list of lifesaving things that he could choose to be or not be done if he was almost dead. *Yeah, what am I now? I don't think so.*

"I want all the stuff to keep me going that's on here, the whole enchilada. Don't pull the plug."

"Pete, will you at least take a few minutes to think it through?"

"What else do I have to do but think about this shit? I'm a *survivor*. End of story!" he shouted, slamming his fist on the table for good measure.

Instinctively, Kathy drew back, hands up in front of her. It was rare to see him angry these days. A weapon that had cowed the whole family, his rage had abated as he'd gotten sicker and sicker.

"Okay," she said quietly. "I get it. So, now we need to get this notarized if you want them to do all this stuff. I mean: if it should ever come to that."

He's scared shitless about what's happening to him, alone except for me, Becca, and, marginally, Corina, she thought. *Friends? What friends he'd had were gone. Probably in jail. Or wasted. Or dead.*

"Sorry I got a little heated," he said, confounding her again by actually making an apology. "It's just, all this waiting for the transplants."

"Umm..." It took her a few beats to get what he was talking about. Transplants? Plural, as in new kidney and a liver? Maybe throw in a heart? *Oh, Pete, what planet are you on? There's like a 0.0001 chance for that. At this stage of the game, you'd probably die on the operating table, and, anyway, it would not get that far. A pipe dream—maybe literally? Was he smoking again? Weed was like pablum for an old doper like Pete.*

They came back to the apartment after they'd gotten the paperwork signed and witnessed and stamped at the bank. Kathy had thought it would be nice to stop at a café for coffee or iced tea, but Pete said he was exhausted from the effort.

How the hell would he manage in Mexico for three days?

Well, he'll be at the beach. He doesn't have to do *anything there.*

As she drove through the thick afternoon traffic, she marveled once again at her brother's capacity for self-deception. Pete, who had nothing of his own (well, his mystery music);

Pete, who had cirrhosis and diabetes and had had two heart attacks and wasn't even fifty yet; this Pete wanted his life to go on no matter what. And yes, she had to respect that. He'd always been delusional, but you had to kind of admire someone who, despite all the suffering, the bleakness, wanted to stay alive no matter what.

CHAPTER 10

The koi seemed to dart more energetically, more nervously than usual in the small backyard pond shaded by ferns. Becca wondered if the fish were picking up on her vibes. She angled the smoke from her long-stashed pack of Marlboro Lights away from it. She felt like a brittle stick, ready to snap.

The beauty around her, most of which she had created, usually helped her, like the calm of an aquarium at a hospital. But her oasis (she tried not to remind herself it was infinitesimal compared to Corina's backyard) could have been paved in concrete for all the good it was doing her today. She thought about her last argument with Cam, when she'd been right to be afraid of him. She knew she'd never forget the shock when her child hit her on the face. The bruise on her cheek, red then blue then a sickening chartreuse. Finally a dusty brown. "Oh, a stupid fall," she'd say to nosy neighbors, pretending to laugh about her clumsiness. *Like a domestic abuse victim*, her brain whispered. A sense of shame never left her—or Toby, now. *All the things we've done for him. And nothing has helped. We've failed.*

She made herself watch the blood-orange fish in their tiny sea, but for once she took no pleasure from their graceful turns or their flowerlike markings or the green border that shaded the pond. Not even the peaceful splash of the tiny waterfall helped. She wondered if she'd forgotten to feed the fish again. She couldn't bear it if they died, or if Denby snuck out of the house again and killed them. He'd done that to their predecessors, though he hadn't bothered to eat them. Had they sensed his feline terrorist presence; had they frozen in their circling? On the other hand, wasn't it natural? Predator and prey. She peered at the pond as she shook in fish food. It was getting murky, she realized.

"What are you *doing*?" Toby demanded a few minutes later.

Becca whipped her head around, the only body part she could move while stretched over the koi pool, balancing with one hand on a rock. She pushed herself up and away, in the process dropping the net she'd been holding to scoop scum with her other hand from the water.

"What does it look like? What a novel situation! The fish pond is full of slime, but nobody bothers to clean it. Except me, surprise. I can't even imagine the state of Denby's litter box." She sat on the gravel path and began to weep, as much for her sharpness—bitchiness—with Toby as for Cam, never mind herself.

Toby, who knew her moods better, almost, than she did, led her to the wicker chairs nearby. They both slumped down.

"Phil will be here again any minute," he said.

She looked at him blankly.

"That leak in the roof," he reminded her.

"Well, darn it, he'll just have to see a couple of broken-down wrecks. He's used to us by now."

Toby tried to touch her face. She snapped away as if he were about to attack her.

"I'm sorry," she whispered. "I can't be around anyone right now."

"Except those fucking fish." He stood up.

"They can't talk back to me," she said.

"You don't let anybody talk back to you," Toby said and went back inside.

Becca resumed cleaning the pond. She collected herself—that was her mother's phrase, "collect yourself, girls"—and mentally rummaged through her kitchen. She'd cook for Toby in penance. The freezer was well-stocked, the fridge stuffed. The cornucopia was always filled, even when the coffers were low. Another of Julia's rules: always have something on hand in case people drop by.

However, when she inspected it, the fridge was nearly bare. Was she losing her mind? She remembered then. Since Cam had been "sent away" five days before, neither she nor Toby had shopped or bothered with anything more than scratch meals and takeout. Takeout again tonight, then, though the budget was getting more out of whack. And Phil wouldn't care if she didn't offer him a snack. He'd be happy with a glass of water.

But she could do better than that: she would make iced tea, crush in a few mint leaves, do the hostess thing. Then retire to her study at the top of the house. And meditate. Well, brood. The point was, she'd sit *quietly*.

Working on her poetry was out of the question right now in the wake of the latest chapter of the catastrophe of Cam. Those who knew her well, and there weren't many, thought of Becca as fully competent to handle life. Manager at Barnaby's Frames & More, devoted mother, wife, sister, poems published (several, in little magazines). But now that Cam had been spirited off to the rehab in the middle of the night, a rehab dubbed a "wilderness center," Becca didn't have it in her to do anything after she cleaned the koi pond. She reminded herself that soon, she'd be off to Rincón Bay with the sibs.

If she hadn't seen her reflection in the glass of the open door to the petite dining room, she wouldn't have realized she grimaced as she thought this.

CHAPTER 11

The neurologist, Dr. Oakman, a fleshy man, looked up sharply from his desk as Corina burst through the door.

"Mrs. Swanson, isn't it? Please, take a deep breath. Here's a tissue."

"Not Swanson! I won't use his name ever again!"

A nurse sidled in and raised her eyebrows. "Everything all right, Doctor?"

"We're just a little upset. Shut the door as you leave, would you, Karen? Ms. . . . uh, take a seat. Just breathe in and out, would you, please."

"I don't want to breathe," Corina said, but she sat down.

Dr. Oakman gave her another sharp look, then busied himself with her chart. "And I understand that you're here because you disagree with your diagnosis?" he asked eventually.

"Because I don't know what's wrong with me and nobody else does either."

He tapped the paperwork, frowning. She was crying, hiccupping sobs. The doctor pressed a buzzer, and the nurse came back in. "Would you get the lady a glass of water?

"Mrs. S—uh." He paused, frowned. "You've had a thorough workup. I'm concerned, though, about these mood swings."

"He wants to take the house from me," Corina said between sobs. "How would you feel if you had to leave your home?"

Nurse Karen, who had returned with the water, patted her shoulder as Dr. Oakman leaned forward. "Now, now, Mrs. uh—is it Talley now?" He tapped her file. "You see, what concerns me are the mood swings," he repeated.

"But Dr. Lorber says—"

He waved a hand. "More hard evidence, that's what's needed. Now, I want to run some tests."

Corina jumped up and her chair fell back, striking Karen in the shin. "No more tests! I can't!" She began to wail and abruptly sat down on the floor.

"Karen! Are you all right?"

"Just a slight bruise, Doctor."

"Please get up off the floor, Mrs. Swanson, uh, Talley."

Corina shook her head. "No, I can't go on like this!" But she leaped to her feet, throwing out her arms as she did so and, this time, struck the nurse in the face.

Dr. Oakman, furious about having his office hijacked by a hysterical and potentially violent patient—twice now she'd lashed out at his nurse—decided he had a "10-56 A" code on his hands. He dialed the police.

Afterward, when Corina related the fragments of what she remembered of what followed, it seemed far-fetched, fantastic. And Corina was, well, given to flights of fancy now. But Imalia, in the waiting room, had witnessed the two silent cops who appeared, grim-faced and in a hurry, emerging shortly from an office with a flailing, whimpering Corina, and she followed them at a cautious distance to the parking lot, where she watched them put her employer in a police car.

Then she called Kathy. She was too upset to speak in English and hoped Kathy got the gist.

Kathy, who did, called Dr. Lorber, who was in a session but called her back soon after.

"What on earth? The police? What happened? And why did Corina go to *him*? She already has a neurologist. Now, did this man look at the assessment?"

"I don't know exactly..."

Dr. Lorber sighed heavily. "I'll call him and find out where she is. And then I'm going to give him a large piece of my mind."

But Dr. Lorber got Oakman's voicemail. He didn't get back to her until that evening, and they ended up hanging up on each other.

Then Dr. Lorber called Kathy to let her know that Corina was in Pima County Psychiatric Hospital on a mandatory twenty-four-hour hold.

The next afternoon, in the middle of teaching a class at the community college, Kathy's phone buzzed. She recognized Dr. Lorber's number and stepped into the hall to call her back. Then she called Becca. "The psych hospital is releasing Corina. Can you come with me to get her?"

After ending the class early, Kathy drove to Barnaby's Frames & More. There was a short delay while Becca organized a replacement; then they headed for the part of Tucson they never went to, populated largely by dollar stores; taco, auto-repair, and check-cashing shops; and the old hospital that loomed over the seedy landscape, equally run-down.

To Kathy, the ugly bland building seemed to be floating in the scorching heat that bleached the air.

"I think I'm still in shock," she told Becca, cutting the engine in the parking lot.

"Me too, it's a nightmare," Becca said with a slow shake of her head.

They went inside, were frisked, and were told to wait in the depressing lobby with the ubiquitous hard plastic chairs such places provide. An hour went by before Corina appeared, shuffling toward them.

"Take me away from here!" she said hoarsely.

In the hot car, Kathy blasted the air conditioning, which feebly attacked the heat. It was another oven-like day in the desert, where you had to wear gloves when you first touched car surfaces. Kathy dug out water bottles from a little cooler. They all drank with abandon.

"Are you okay?" Becca ventured.

"No," Corina said in a flat tone that indicated she was highly medicated. "Some woman with the worst red dye job made me take this pill that knocked me out, and then another woman woke me up and gave me a chicken sandwich. And orange juice. And another pill. Could I have a latte?"

"What? In a minute. Didn't you see a doctor?"

"Maybe. Not Dr. Lorber. I want a latte."

Kathy, mind on fire with outrage, drove out of the shabby parking lot of the psych hospital to look for a coffee spot.

After they got coffee at a drive-through, Kathy parked in some shade. She turned to look at Corina in the back seat.

"Why did you go to some random doctor? Dr. Lorber's there for you, from what you've told me."

Corina flinched as if she had been hit. "I don't know!"

"We're just trying to understand...the...situation," Becca said soothingly.

"Because I got a letter from Tom. He's getting married again. I got so angry." Corina took a sip. "I really needed something to calm me down. Dr. Lorber said to take another Ativan, but it didn't help. I just...I felt crazy. So Imalia and I googled neurologists and that guy had an opening."

"Okay," Kathy said with a sigh. "Well, that's over. And just ignore the letter. Who cares what that shit does?"

Kathy and Becca exchanged looks. It was so unlike Corina, always meticulous about health care providers, to go to some random doctor. *But, that was the old Corina,* she reminded herself, feeling a twist of the familiar pain in her chest. Corina! She certainly was not fading away, as Kathy had naively assumed would happen with dementia. No, she was fighting a war in which pieces of her crashed and burned around her—and everybody else.

"We can sue that moth—man," she said.

"No! I just want peace and quiet!"

"Ah, that," Kathy said.

"Don't we all," Becca said. "Peace and quiet."

CHAPTER 12

"**W**hat?" Pete said, answering his phone.

"It's me. Calling to see what the nutritionist said."

"All good, Kath."

"Did you get the new meal-delivery plan set up? Because . . . it's important, you know."

"Yes! Jeez! I'm kinda tired. Talk to you later. Bye."

Pete tossed his phone on the coffee table (Julia's) and pulled himself up out of the Barcalounger. He needed a shower. Had needed one for a day or two but he got so tired. People—Kathy—just didn't understand. She was always on him about something, this new bug up her ass, the super-duper deluxe diabetic food plan. She meant well, but she had no clue. It was a chore to eat, to tell the truth.

He kicked the chair and, ignoring his body odor, limped lightly into his studio.

With his new DAWless sampler and sequencer setup, he had no need for a computer. He was back in business. So much easier. Mind-blowing, the music he could make with his analog synthesizer, drum machine, mic, mixer, and now the DAWless. A miracle, that he'd held on to his equipment all these years since practically everyone he'd associated with was a junkie and/or a thief. But he had defended his kingdom of music-making, hadn't he? So maybe there had to be a bit of kicking ass at times. And several times, he'd changed the locks on the trailer. During that last really bad bit, when he got too involved with substances again, he'd persuaded Kathy to move his gear into her garage, though he practically had to get down on his knees before she'd agree. Then, once he got this apartment, his sisters and their husbands (except Tom, who never did anything approaching manual labor as a point of honor, declaring he was done with all that after a childhood on a farm), had helped move everything in. Since then, he hadn't let anybody else touch his equipment.

Pete forced himself to switch mental gears and psych himself up to work on his new song, a country-rock drum groove with Captain Beefheart–inspired lyrics.

> I may be dying but you are too.
> I may be crying, boo-hoo-hoo.
> But I'm gonna tell my story till the bitter end
> And you may not like it when I go 'round the bend
> 'Cause I may be dying. But you are too.

Pete was in his bliss.

CHAPTER 13

Each time Imalia slid into her blue Camry and started it up, first she automatically blessed Señor Tom for his generosity. Then, without any sense of contradiction, she added *el rato*, because Señor Tom *was* a rat for what he'd done to the señora.

One day, Imalia had shown up for work drenched from a (rare, blessed) cloudburst. Her commute to the Swansons' *casa grande* involved two long bus rides from her sister Luchita's house, culminating in the steep walk up the hill from the gates of the complex. When she came in the house dripping, it was Tom, sitting at the breakfast bar, who jumped up and got her a towel. And not many days later, he ushered her into the garage, spreading out his hands at the used Toyota Camry parked beside Corina's Mercedes SUV. Used but pristine.

Tom handed her a set of keys. "It's yours!"

Imalia didn't know how to drive, but Tom had organized that too. He informed her that a driving instructor would come that very afternoon to begin her lessons. Neither of them brought up the fact that she was illegal. (So what? So was half the town.)

"Oh, Señor Tom." She began to cry.

"The least I can do for you. That or an umbrella."

She knew it was true. She did far more than keep house. She listened to Señora Corina, she consoled her, she made comforting pozoles and Mexican hot chocolate. It didn't matter that Imalia didn't understand much of what the increasingly unhappy señora said. She got that the beautiful, high-strung señora was sad and lonely. Which wasn't a wonder at all to Imalia because she knew from her telenovelas that the rich were like this, always dissatisfied despite having a dream life. Too much time on their hands!

It also wasn't a wonder to Imalia that her señora complained about Señor Tom, the source of her great good fortune. *Así son los machos*, she was tempted to tell her employer: That's what men are like, the center, as they think, of the world. At that time, she did not know for certain about the señor's other women, but the señora eventually let that cat out of the bag along with her other woes. Imalia thought again, *He's rich, what do you expect?* But how Señora Corina suffered from his longer and longer absences, and when he was around, his jokey, gift-bearing ways couldn't hide his coldness to her.

So, though she was paid well by her standards, had even been given a car, Imalia began to detest Señor Tom as the señora became so *flaca* in body and mind. Did he not see this? How could he treat her so? Imalia began thinking of him as *el rato*. A man who didn't care that his wife suffered because of him.

Yet how she loved her Camry! For the first time in her nearly forty years, Imalia could go where she wanted and do what she wanted, so easily! Shop, bingo, mass every now and then, and Lola's Cantina more and more often—religiously, you could say. She didn't care to think of going back to the *patria*. Luchita was anxious to go because of the bad habits that had caught up with Papi, that old string bean clinging to the rocky soil of the ranchito, his little crops and his goats, their brother Lucho, another *rato*, sponging off of him, and Marci, his ghost of a wife, and their kids, who should get out of there like half of Mexico as soon as they could.

"*Es nuestra responsabilidad, Imi,*" Luchita told her sister continually. But Imalia put it off, though they now had their papers. And yet she yearned for certain things about Mexico, the sharp smell of the mountains, the taste of real *Norteño* food, even hearing Papi's raspy voice. And the chickens as they scratched around, making sounds she equated with peace. Señor Tom had been as good as his word about helping her get legal, after she was given the Camry. She had to be forever grateful to him, but she was glad when the señora stopped dithering around, got the divorce, and kicked him out of the house.

Señora Corina had decided it was time to clean out the clothes closets again. It might have been a simple undertaking for some, but for Corina, it was anything but that. There were—still—dozens of gowns, dresses, skirts, shoes, bags, belts, jackets, coats, sweaters, pants, shirts, tops, scarves—some in duplicate.

Imalia was, of course, deputized to sort, bag, discard. Not that there would be much, in the end, to get rid of. Señora Corina never liked to part with things.

"We'll do a major weeding today, Imalia," her employer promised, as she always did, when they began. Imalia thought she'd said "wedding," a word she knew, and which made sense to her: all those fancy dresses, enough for a plethora of quinceañeras. From experience, though, she knew it would be a marathon without a finish line. Señora Corina was a world-class ditherer; each item seemed to inspire a story that Imalia's passable English was sometimes just good enough to catch the gist of.

"And there I was—isn't this gorgeous, Imalia?—feel this silk—on my *wedding day*, which should be the happiest day of your life, next to having kids, and yes, I'd had some champagne and so I had to pee. I go to our bathroom off the bedroom and what do I find? There he is, snorting coke off the counter! After he promised he wouldn't anymore, it was one of our conditions. And I could see it wasn't the first line that day. His eyes glittering like glass. But what does he say? 'Hey, Corina! Want some?' No, I did not want some, I wanted him to keep his promise." She handed Imalia the beautiful dress, a shimmering, silvery blue. "This one is for that really good thrift shop downtown."

Imalia folded it carefully. She understood that it was too nice for a quinceañera.

So it went. Slowly, slowly: the really good pile, the good pile, the Salvation Army pile, the giveaways to Imalia, and the trash pile.

"Everything size 4 or more goes," Corina added belatedly. Now that she was down to a 00.

Imalia waited, folding and refolding the little piles. It was taking so long, and she had things to do, after all. The kitchen to clean, the dinner to prep. And she wanted to get home today in time to watch *La Casa de las Flores*, her favorite show. Above all, to get out of this room, a claustrophobic closetful of sadness.

Corina suddenly sat down on the floor among the piles. "Oh, what am I doing? I used to have a life. All the parties and places..." Her eyes were huge and soft, pale brown lit by pale yellow, like a distant candle burning. "And before that, you know, I worked. I worked hard. *Yo era trabajadora social,*" she said proudly in a hard American accent. "I did some good."

"You are good person, Señora Corina."

"I should have kept on working. I really liked my job. Why did I stop?"

"You have *la familia,*" Imalia reminded her.

"Oh, yes. *Familia.*"

Now, Imalia thought, comes the crying. There were more *lágrimas* in this woman than anyone she knew.

But for once, Corina didn't cry. In a small voice she said, "Oh, let's quit now. *You* are the social worker now, Imalia, helping me so much."

"I help," Imalia admitted.

She seldom thought about her own lost career, but as she drove home later—half an hour after her telenovela had begun—she allowed herself to wonder what her life would be now, if she hadn't left Mexico.

In Hermosillo, the capital of the state of Sonora, where the sisters Imalia and Luchita Ortiz were sent to live after their mother died, Tía Rosalia arranged everything. She cajoled and bribed Luchita into a good *primaria* and, being four years older, Imalia into a *preparatoria* that focused on job training. Coming from a village where school was a joke, Imalia was overwhelmed, but with her aunt's tutoring, she soon caught up. And she made a friend.

Valentina was a spunky girl one year older who was focusing on hospitality, hoping to get a job in a tourist hotel at Rincón Bay up north on the Sea of Cortez, or maybe in Baja, and Imalia was enchanted by Valentina's ambition—and by Valentina. She decided she would do the same. She had had no idea of making a future for herself other than life on the ranchito before she came to Hermosillo. She told Tía Rosalia about her plans, who nodded her head. "Better to have a good job and then (her aunt crossed herself), meet a good man."

Imalia pictured herself behind a desk in one of those crisp uniforms in the palace-like hotels she'd seen in brochures at the *preparatoria*. And next to her, identically dressed, would be shorter, raven-haired Valentina.

Imalia was in love, a secret she kept to herself. But Luchita sensed there was someone and begged her to tell her who it was. Lying in the bed they shared in the narrow room that had been filled with cans and sacks before they arrived, Luchita wheedled and whined, but Imalia would not say.

"Don't let him do that thing boys want, Imi, you might end up pregnant!" Luchita advised anyway.

Imalia smiled in the dark, thinking of her darling Vale. "You don't know what you're talking about. You're only eleven. And stop sticking your nose in my business or I'll tear up your homework."

No, there was no chance of Imalia getting pregnant.

It seemed to her that the crisis the next year, which wrenched her and Luchita from their new life in Hermosillo with its tantalizing possibilities, happened with lightning speed. But in fact, it unspooled over months. The ache in Tía Rosalia's chest got worse, finally sending her with great reluctance to the neighborhood *clínica*, where lumps in her left breast and under her arm were found and she was directed to the small but thriving cancer hospital for treatment that only postponed her death by several months.

Imalia's father did not come to get his girls when his wife's sister died; he never left the vicinity of the ranchito. It was their brother Lucho who came. Since Tía Rosalia was a widow without heirs, he loaded up the old pickup with her belongings, the table, chairs, a mattress, linens, and crockery. The girls were to sit in the back with the stuff for the trip into the mountains. But they had decided not to go back with Lucho. No matter how much he threatened. When he lunged at Imalia, she and Luchita ran inside the tiny house and bolted the door.

Eventually, after several minutes of shouting and cursing, Lucho took off. He was probably relieved, Imalia thought.

They stayed because they had a plan, or Imalia did. When Tía Rosalia knew she was dying, she'd told her nieces where she'd hidden her money, acquired in dribs and drabs over the years for what she had dreamed would be a trip to Tucson, Arizona, where she had many relatives. "Now it will be for you. I cannot help you anymore. You must find your future over there with the family. So what you are to do is ask around for a Señor Alfredo. The neighbors will know who you mean. He knows the coyotes who can get you over the border. But don't tell him how much money there is or he'll rob you blind."

They were amazed to find stacks of pesos in a tin under a board, the equivalent then of around five hundred dollars. It was a lot of money, more than enough to get them over the border, over to the place called Tucson. They had never had more than a few pesos in their pockets before.

The night before they were to meet the coyotes, Imalia met Valentina in the little plaza behind the San Peregrino church, where few people passed, to say goodbye. She was determined not to break down and cry but as soon as they sat down, side by side, hands clasped tightly under the folds of Valentina's purple skirt, Imalia began to sob. Valentina was dry-eyed. She said, "Don't go," and squeezed Imalia's hands so hard with her own that Imalia stopped crying, afraid Valentina would make a scene, right there on the iron bench festooned with pigeon droppings, though no one was around but some old drunk on the other side of the little square.

But Valentina became quite calm as she lobbed verbal grenades. "You leave me now and I will never speak your name again," she said. "I will erase you from my life like a stain from a blouse."

Then Imalia was the one who made a scene. "I am not leaving you!" she said in a very loud and ragged voice she did not recognize. "I am only going because we have no way to survive here now. You know it's true. You can come to Tucson" (she pronounced it "Tuksoon," a logical error) "when I get a job there."

"It doesn't work like that! You don't have papers. What do you think? They will put you in jail, then throw you back over the border!" Valentina stood up suddenly, wrenching her hands from Imalia's hot ones. Her blue blouse and her deep-purple skirt looked black in the darkness, for the streetlamps were almost all broken. "*Nunca me olvides.*" She stalked away, and Imalia stayed on the bench as if pinned there. *Never forget me.*

The next day at dawn, Imalia and Luchita began their journey to the strange new land.

CHAPTER 14

Imalia turned her back for a few moments, and Corina was out the door.

She ran down Cabo Gordo Street in the now-dingy kimono she'd bought in Kyoto for an immense sum during an around-the-world business-class trip to Japan, Cape Town, Sri Lanka, Vietnam, and somewhere else that Tom sprang on her for her fortieth birthday.

She got only two blocks away before Imalia caught up with her.

"I have to get away from here!" Corina announced when Kathy answered the phone.

"You are getting away. We're going to the beach soon. Remember?"

"Oh. The beach. It's so . . . I can't think of the word."

"Calming?"

"Yes. Are we going to Puerto Vallarta?"

"We'd have to fly and we can't do that," Kathy reminded her.

"Oh."

"We're driving to Rincón Bay, remember?"

Corina gasped. "But you hate that place!"

Kathy said carefully, "I'm sure it's very different since I was there. Probably unrecognizable, all built up." *Yes, please let them have bulldozed and paved over those scrubby dunes. Installed tacky margarita bars. Taco stands. Souvenir shops.*

"We'd better hurry up. Before Pete dies," Corina said.

"Well, let's not get into that."

"He's got cirrhosis and something else that's horrible," Corina said, with an odd lack of affect. "I think I'll probably need help too," she added.

Kathy felt the familiar hammer-like kick to her gut. "Imalia's coming."

Though it had taken some convincing and bribery.

"If you're worried about ICE," Kathy had said to Imalia, "don't. You're a legal resident. Besides, it's a vacation. You'll have a lot of time to yourself."

Imalia had been silent.

"Of course, you'll have your own room at the hotel." Inspiration struck at last. "Plus, a bonus."

Imalia, who had acquired an impressive English vocabulary about practical things—above all money—had finally agreed.

Pete blamed himself. Dumb. Obviously, the cop—your standard, beefy white guy with a buzz cut—thought so too. He shook his head and was probably rolling his eyes behind his biker sunglasses, as he flipped open his notebook.

"So, sir, what were you thinking here?" The cop pointed at the car ahead, its bumper tilted like a metal noodle. "I got to breathalyze you. Blow in here."

Pete said, "I'm COPD," and proceeded to show him the card in his wallet attesting to that. He showed his dialysis card too. The cop, used to sick old codgers crawling around the streets of Tucson, sighed. Wearily, he started filling in his paperwork.

It was the glare of the Arizona sun that had temporarily thrown him. The car he'd hit was being driven by a little old lady—one of the many similar throwbacks who'd migrated here, in the uniform of white hair, baggy jeans, some kind of flowery blouse, and thick white sneakers—who now paced unsteadily nearby. Not hurt, as far as Pete could tell, but she kept shooting him sideways angry looks.

The cop turned a fraction and advised her the process would take a while. "Why don't you go sit down on the bench outside the dollar store in the shade?" he suggested in a nicer tone of voice than he'd used with Pete.

Kathy had been nagging him to get rid of the car, Mom's old—really old—Buick Park Avenue, which Pete had inherited. Julia had maintained it meticulously, rarely drove it in the last years of her life, but he'd put a lot of miles on it. Kathy said it was a financial liability. One, it was a guzzler, and two, his insurance had skyrocketed due to several previous accidents he'd had, just fender benders like this one, but still. He had agreed to get rid of it. *But come on, give me a break*, he mentally rehearsed in his defense to her, *a man needs wheels in this town. And you girls haven't exactly suggested springing for a replacement, have you?*

As the policeman wrote out the ticket, Pete looked again at the lady he'd dinged, parked now on the bench, and it seemed to him that she took on the outlines of his mother. She had Julia's vibe of being there but not there, outwardly submissive but inwardly defiant.

"What? Yes, sir. Yes, I will," Pete responded to the cop's order that he pay his fine promptly. He was still engrossed in thinking of his mom.

"Okay, fine," he addressed the Buick when he got in. "Fuck it, I'm getting rid of you."

The next day when Kathy phoned—he called it his daily "Mom call"—he told her he'd gotten rid of the car.

"I thought you did that like three months ago."

"I wasn't *driving* it." Much. The only trip he'd taken longer than a run to the dialysis center or Walmart was back to the trailer park to visit Bert, because Bert had called and said he was back from rehab and why didn't they hang out? Bert's girlfriend Stacy didn't like Pete, but tough shit.

That day Pete had maneuvered the car slowly, maybe a bit high from the extra oxy he'd taken because his back was acting up, but without incident. He and Bert and Stacy went to a nearby park, where Bert offered him a beer from the six-pack he'd brought, but Pete said he'd have water. He did share a j with them at the picnic table where they ate the turkey sandwiches Stacy had slapped together until a lady with some little kids at the next table came over and yelled at them about the j. They went back to the trailer and sat outside Bert's place in lawn chairs and shot the shit and Bert got so loaded he fell asleep.

As soon as that happened, Stacy went inside and Pete went for a walk around the trailer park. He found he had no nostalgia for this place where he'd lived for twelve years. It was full of trash and poor Mexicans or whatever who never stopped blasting their Norteño crap. He went back and woke up Bert and said he had to go. Bert tried to get him to "loan" him some money. "You got a rich sister, bro, I got squat." They got into an argument when Pete refused, and then Bert said fuck you.

"Fine," Kathy was saying. "Well, speaking of driving, our trip to Mexico's coming right up. So, start packing."

"Hey, hey," he said.

"Pete. Are you high? You sound high on something."

As far as he was concerned, he was stone-cold sober. He had cool-turkeyed (his little joke) all the other stuff. He felt that his current condition was the "sobriety" that Becca especially, and okay, yeah, the doctors, had whined on at him about. Suggesting he go to AA. Like he was going to join a cult.

"Nah, I'm just tired." But hell, maybe she was right. He was fuzzy. His tolerance all gone to shit. *That's what dialysis does for you*, he thought.

He must have chuckled then because she said, "You *are* stoned."

"About this trip. I gotta be at dialysis every three days."

Kathy sighed. "I told you, we'll get you back for Monday afternoon. Pete?" Long pause. "You still there?"

"Yeah, well, I didn't know it was such a quick trip."

"Well, I told you."

He covered the phone and let out a shuddering sob. "Listen," he said huskily, "I gotta go. Call you back later."

"*Fucking walking dead!*" Last words he'd heard as he got in the car, though Bert was still screaming at him as he floored the Buick and screeched out of the trailer park. Why had that popped up in his head now?

Because that's what you are, asshole, the baleful part of his brain growled at him.

CHAPTER 15

Corina was feeling better. Dr. Lorber had tweaked her meds yet again and she wasn't so restless. She was sitting on the patio with the fan blowing, binoculars focused on the brown patch of lawn.

Imalia approached with a pitcher of ice water with slices of orange in it, the way Corina liked, along with her cell phone. "Phone, Señora Corina."

Corina shook her head. "Not now, Imalia. Henrique's playing hide-and-seek."

"It's your sister, Mrs. Kathy," Imalia insisted. "She says is important."

Corina sighed, as if much was being asked of her, and slowly removed the binoculars. "Yes? What is it, Kathy?" she said briskly.

"Oh, am I interrupting something?"

"I'm watching Henrique. Oh, he waved one of his legs. He's so cute. Now he's climbing on a rock."

"Rock on, Henrique," Kathy said, but Corina heard the sigh on the other end of the line.

"Listen, Corina, I got us a place in Rincón. We're leaving Friday right after Pete's dialysis, at two sharp."

"To Puerto Vallarta?"

"No! Rincón Bay. You, me, Becca, Pete, and Imalia."

"What about Bernard and Toby?" She was proud of herself for remembering their names.

"Nope, just us sibs."

"I haven't packed." Even in the best of times, Corina had always struggled with this part of travel. So many choices!

"There's plenty of time. Imalia will help. Just simple beach stuff. All you need is a swimsuit, T-shirts, shorts, some flip-flops. Maybe a skirt, a pair of pants. And a hat. Completely casual. Sunscreen, of course."

"But what about Henrique? I can't abandon him." The tortoise had lived for years in her large, enclosed backyard, the lush plantings providing ample hiding places and leaves to munch on, though of course she provided top-of-the-line feed from the boutique pet store near the mall. She fussed over his diet, his well-being, his recreational opportunities, even his need—maybe—for a mate. *And he only just reappeared!* she reminded herself. *How can I leave him now?*

"Your tortoise, turtle, whatever, will be fine. He has all that grass and stuff to eat. It's just three days."

Maybe Kathy was right. Henrique, though clearly appreciative of the organic mesclun she left for him on flat rocks, did seem perfectly content on his own.

"Okay," she agreed tentatively. "Since it's just a short trip."

Kathy let out another lusty sigh as she hung up the phone, which coincided with Bernard wandering into the kitchen.

"What's up?"

"Oh, you know. Corina." Kathy looked up. "She used to be so full of life!"

"That she was. The high life."

"All she cares about now is Henrique."

His eyebrows shot up. "What, she has a boyfriend?"

"No! Her desert turtle. Tortoise, I mean."

"Oh right. All good with the trip?"

"Well, I hope it's a good idea."

Bernard peeled a banana, sliced it, and ate. "You know how I feel about it."

"I hate it when you talk while you're eating."

He swallowed. "I'm just saying. I don't get it. You refused to go when the kids begged us to. And those two? The shape they're in?" He shrugged. "Waste of breath, though, since when do you listen to me?"

"Bernard!"

CHAPTER 16

Bernard and Toby were at the Freakness, their usual hangout two blocks from the campus. As the name implied, the place had been around a long time. And it didn't seem to have changed much since the 1970s. The two claimed they liked it because it was close to the campus, but it was really the nostalgia thing, though Bernard wasn't yet in his teens back then and Toby was born in the 1970s. They always sat in the game room, quieter than the main bar with the loud jukebox that featured, yes, Hendrix and Cream, but also a lot of old-school blues. Plus, they could play pool.

Bernard and Toby had met when both were newly married but hadn't started hanging until Toby and Becca left New York, where they were among the countless number of struggling artists with college degrees who scraped by with dumb jobs and crappy apartments. Bernard, an adjunct then at the university, had helped get Toby a one-year teaching contract in the music department on the strength of his book *History of Rockabilly*, which Toby managed to parlay into an ongoing gig. Toby and Bernard became friends, evenly matched, which is to say not very good at pickup basketball games at the university. And it helped that they had similar tastes in books and movies. But what they really enjoyed was sharpening their wits on their differences in music, a major passion. Bernard, to Toby's purported shock, couldn't abide doo-wop and Toby didn't like much jazz except Miles and Brubeck.

"Man, you look stressed-out," Toby said, setting their bottles of Carlsbad on the table they liked against the back wall. "*Without Walls* not progressing?"

"I can't seem to find a way to wrap it up." Even more than Kathy, Toby knew the twists and turns of Bernard's book.

"You're coming to the finish line, always tough," Toby said.

"I'm not having much luck with the pitch I'm working on."

Bernard tilted his bottle at Toby. "Remind me again?" Toby had had so many irons in the fire. And unfortunately, none of them had ignited for a few years.

"The doc about folk-rock so-called obscurities. Jim and Jean? Tim Rose? The Stone Poneys, at least, should clinch it."

"Young Linda Ronstadt? Yeah, that should play to the suits."

They fell silent, concentrated on their beers.

On the second round, Bernard began to get confessional. "I don't know, man, I don't know." He shook his head. "Feels like everything's up in the air right now. Way up."

"You should have been a shoo-in for the fucking chair."

Bernard shook his head again. "I don't really care about that. All that admin shit. The money would have been useful of course. But it's not that. It's that they picked *him*."

He paused, drank. That morning he'd gotten up early, as usual. Kathy liked to sleep in; he didn't. Make some coffee, go for a run before it gets hot. As he was pulling on his shorts, he happened to turn and noticed how the early morning light lit up her hair in its tangled waves and—it was as if he'd either not noticed before or immediately sublimated it—he saw that her hair was no longer that soft brown. Had all that gray invaded overnight? And not the silver fox kind. He pulled a T-shirt over his head then looked at her again. Lying on her stomach with an arm flung outside the covers, the skin slightly saggy. Damn, she was showing her age! He had the crazy thought of tipping her over and examining the rest of her.

In the bathroom mirror, he examined his face closely. His father, old-school, had told him he was "a yellow." But no, he was a Black man by the rules of American colorism, his skin rich in melanin, repelling UV rays. Which meant fewer wrinkles. "Black don't crack," as the old saying went. Unlike his wife's. Okay, there *was* some sagging on him. His legs were like rocks and his arms were good, but that was definitely a little pouch there on his midriff. And was his hair thinning? He wasn't sure. Which probably meant it was.

"You know," he said to Toby now, "we've been with the same women about the same amount of time."

Toby nodded. "Two strong-ass sisters."

Bernard liked Becca, despite her prickliness, and knew Toby liked Kathy; he liked her art, especially the subversively whimsical drawings, which he had urged her, without success yet, to submit to *The New Yorker*. But Toby didn't seem interested in talking about wives right now, so Bernard's rare urge to confide passed.

"Another one for the road?" Toby said.

"Sure."

While Toby went to get the beer, Bernard studied his hands on the table, the hands of a pianist, large and broad with long tapered fingers. But he didn't play, he *listened*. And he wrote about it. It had disappointed him, and his father probably even more, that he didn't have the chops to become a player. Well, that was over a long time ago.

When Toby came back, Bernard took a deep drink as if he were parched, and then he couldn't help himself talking about Kathy. "She's so fucking *driven*. Every cause. Black Lives Matter, brown, pink, purple." He thought he seldom talked about her this directly. Directly negatively, he corrected himself. Should he feel like a shit? He didn't. "Maybe we're in one of those blips, you know, a little *slough of despond* between us." He had another swallow and rallied. "Never mind. Tell me how Cam is doing, that's what's important."

Toby looked away. "I don't know. That's the hell of it. *I don't know*. He's in the middle of nowhere in the mountains, without a cell phone. The place stays in touch with us regularly, of course."

"You did the right thing, sending him there." Bernard tried, once again, to imagine how he'd feel if either of his kids turned out to be addicts. He couldn't imagine it. Tamara had her wobbles, boyfriends mainly, but she was doing well at school, getting her master's in anthropology at Northwestern, so they didn't see her that much anymore. Theo? Not really into academics, but part-time at the U, working. Renting a room in a house with a bunch of guys. Okay, gay guys. Not that far from the Freakness. Involved with some group that helped young runaways, many of whom were gay, or trans, all of whom were in danger. Drawn to helping people. Like his mother. "Anything I can do, you let me know," he told Toby.

They paid up. Both were parked in the university lot and they walked there silently.

At Toby's car, Bernard tapped Toby on the shoulder. Toby tapped him back. Their little ritual.

Toby drove away, the AC off, windows open to the night air, still hot. All he could think about was Cam. Cam, Cam. He had tried to listen to Bernard—he got that Bernard was stressed about the book, Kathy—but there was no room in his head for anything, really, but Cam. Not even Becca. Like Cam was a song you can't get out of your head, a song you both love and hate.

Alone in the car with the breeze and the swish and hum of the traffic, Toby groaned and cursed at the pain that clawed at him. The sleep-defying infant, the rowdy toddler, the always-moving boy, now the lanky seventeen-year-old whose dark curls pushed off his angry forehead. *Maybe I was too understanding, too much of a pal.*

His rejection of that thought was visceral. *No! I was there for him every step of the way!* He pounded the steering wheel. Unlike his dad. His tall and rangy dad, made for basketball. Who rarely tucked him in or read to him at night, whose attention began and ended with how he did on the court. Who, when it became clear that his son would not be a player, switched off.

Toby hated that Cam was not at home, dreaded walking by his son's empty room and not seeing him sprawled across the bed, maybe allowing him to come in for a few minutes. But

Becca had laid it down, and she was right, she was right, God damn it. Cam had to go to treatment, but he would never have gone unless he was forced to.

Toby had made himself go to a couple of those Al-Anon meetings for what Becca called "perspective." He got it, but he wondered if he were a single father if he would have followed her scenario. Paid—a lot—to have two large strangers kidnap his boy in the middle of the night and "escort" him on a plane to the middle of Idaho. Where Cam was to begin what the place called his "sober journey." All Toby wanted was to fold his boy in a bear hug and keep him safe. He was the father, the silverback of their little tribe! And he had failed.

CHAPTER 17

Corina's dream hovered: She and Tom hiking in Colorado, surrounded by the red-gold quivering aspens of late September. She was there—strong, happy, fearless, a fragment of time—and then the dream vaporized as she awoke with an urgent need to pee.

She got up slowly and walked with care to the bathroom she had spent so much time over with the interior designer. The Italian-made double sink, the his-and-her double closets, the jacuzzi, the heavy fittings . . . and as she bent over her sink to rinse her hands and face, Corina saw Tom in her mind, the young Tom in her dream striding through a golden forest. She looked up and saw a haggard face and thinning hair. A strange old woman. Old! She was only fifty-one!

She slammed her fist into the mirror. It vibrated with the impact but didn't shatter. How she wanted to hurt Tom. Seriously fuck him up.

He did this to me!

Imalia found her a bit later, on the huge bed (that was Tom: everything had to be the biggest, the best), cutting up snapshots with a nail scissor.

"The breakfast it is ready, Señora Corina."

"In a minute." She held up a photo. Proud as a kindergartner showing her work. Señor Tom's head was neatly excised from a party shot.

After the señora followed her housekeeper into the kitchen, Imalia asked, "What sweet case you want to take on this trip, the big or little?"

Señora Corina giggled. "It's *suit*case. I need to get a cut and color first." An appointment at the salon had been part of her routine on the many trips of the past: hairdresser, manicurist, a flurry of shopping for last-minute items. "And do I have bathing suits?"

"Yes," Imalia said, though now that her employer had lost so much weight, they were going to be baggy. *Never mind*, she thought. She herself would throw on some shorts and a T-shirt and only get her feet wet when they were at the beach.

"And we need to get Tom some new trunks. I *hate* those Speedos," Señora Corina said. She drained her orange juice.

"Mister Tom? He live in California," Imalia reminded her.

"Oh, that's right," the señora said vaguely, then stood. "I'm going outside to look for Henrique."

Only one bite of toast.

She's disappearing, thought Imalia.

CHAPTER 18

"**Y**ou're comparing a *jazz* musician to Mozart?" The new head of the music department, forty-something, bow-tie-wearing Leo Matterson, leaned back in his chair behind his big new desk, hands behind his head, professorially peering at Bernard through horn-rimmed spectacles. "May I ask why not Beethoven? He's rumored to be a brother."

"That old canard that Beethoven's mother was a Moor?" Bernard shook his head. "Anyway, that's not what this book is about, Leo."

Leo gave him an impassive look. Why, Bernard wondered yet again, had they made *him* the chair? Oh, he knew why, damn it. Matterson checked the boxes: he was Black, he wasn't decrepit, and—key—he was a prolific contributor of reviews, careful prose that wouldn't raise an eyebrow hair of opponents of critical race theory. His book, *Before Fisk: The Music of African American Bands 1807–1883*, was compulsory reading across the land in many music departments, with its exhumations and collations of newspaper accounts, diaries, and so on with mentions of Black church choirs, brass bands, family bands, Civil War bands. It was well-researched, nice and neat and inoffensive, and it had made Matterson a favorite of the old farts in academia who were sick of being accused of not being woke, of being part of the patrimony, of hanging on in the groves past their prime. But the problem with *Before Fisk*, as Bernard saw it, wasn't in the comforting excavation of new, if obscure, Blacks who had made music against all the odds during slavery and the quick backlash after Emancipation. It was the pride that he sensed Leo took, above all, in their assimilation of white cultural expression. But what about the ecstatic ring shouts, the sweat-stained work songs, the down and dirty blues? Bernard would have liked to shout all this at him, but of course, he didn't. Dr. Leo Matterson was his boss now.

"Of course, you're free to write about anything you choose," Leo went on.

Free at last. "You may just learn something when the book is done, Leo," Bernard said to his fellow, and only fellow, Black colleague in the music department.

"See, that's the concern I have. When will we get to see this opus? I understand you've been working on it for—how many years is it again?" For Bernard Barris was respected as a teacher at the university, but, aside from a number of articles over the years—good stuff, mind you—what had he published of consequence? Leo showed him his palms. "And help me clarify this, would you?" he went on. "Exactly what is the book about? Besides a compare and contrast on the Yardbird and Mozart?"

Bernard said nothing. Wuss! Compare and contrast? Worse: calling Charlie Parker *the* Yardbird? Nobody called him that. He was *Yardbird*, mostly just *Bird*. But never mind all that. He had tenure. The new head could make as much noise as he wanted but not much more than that. Bernard worked at repressing both a wince and a scowl.

"And," Leo went on, "I know you say this level of analysis hasn't been done yet on, uh, a jazzman and a classical composer? I am surprised at that, given the *climate* we are in now." Leo leaned forward.

"Well, there have been comparisons, sure, mostly indirect and/or cursory, though," Bernard said. And fuck if he was going to say any more in explanation to this dimwit. *Read the damn book, Leo; that's what it's for.* As for when it would be done, well, he was coming into the home stretch, he felt, even if the last chapter had turned into a shape-shifter, a bone crusher, and his confidence vacillated like a shimmy dancer from a hundred years ago. Late to the party, to complicate matters, he had come to realize that *Music Without Walls* was for his father. A posthumous effort. Bernard Barris Senior, Mechanical Engineer B.S., cum laude, who could not get a job in his field, toiling all his professional life as a glorified clerk, a gofer for other engineers, *white* engineers. The man who had given him a first-class education in music without walls.

"Well, beware the tides of wokeness that threaten to wipe out scholarship, eh, Bernard? Vilification, thy name is woke!" Leo concluded, possibly to his own surprise. Certainly to Bernard's.

And still the man wasn't through!

"What's the title again? Who did you say is publishing it?"

"*Music Without Walls.*"

"Uh-huh. Yeah, what's the sub?" The raison d'etre of academic writing.

Through metaphorically gritted teeth, Bernard said rapidly, "Sub: *The Confluence of Genius of Two* Seemingly *Totally Divergent Artists*. Sub: *The Universality of Cultural Borrowing and Sharing*. Sub: *Everything Is a Construct.*"

"Well, have your little joke, I'm hip," Leo, so clearly not, said. "The publisher?" he asked again. Relentless.

"U of Cal wants it, but a couple others are sniffing around. I'm waiting to see what they might offer."

"Isn't that risky?"

"Wildly." Bernard looked at the time on his phone, stood up abruptly. "Say, Leo, my man, this has been fun. But I have a class to teach. Good talking with you."

Free at last, he thought, walking rapidly away down the hall.

Kathy was in the middle of grading the final papers for Intro to Feminist Art that afternoon when she heard the front door open, then shut.

"I'm back," Bernard announced.

"Hi!" she called out, then continued tapping on her laptop.

Intro to Feminist Art was a class she'd been teaching for seemingly half her life, though really it was about ten years. Adjuncts like her were stuck with the required stuff, and she couldn't possibly refuse the work. Money was money and, thankfully, it was a subject she thought was important, though it no longer fascinated her.

She heard the comforting sounds of a meal being prepped, the refrigerator being opened and closed, water running, a jazz CD playing low on the stereo.

She suspected she was approaching burnout. But she was determined to get all her class work done before leaving for

Rincón Bay; no way did she want to face another cribbed essay about Cindy Sherman or Judy Chicago after the trip.

By the time she'd finished half the pile—surprise, someone had written about Ana Mendieta—dinner smelled ready.

"Hey," she said, shuffling into the kitchen, "it smells good. As usual." She reached over to kiss Bernard on the cheek, but he turned his head.

"Bad day?" she asked, trying not to take the snub personally.

"Bad day," he said. "Up close and personal with Clarence Thomas's doppelgänger."

"Ha ha. Leo. Too bad. Well, I just finished grading ten finals and maybe *three* were college-level. So."

She remembered when they would make each other howl with laughter over life's absurdities. Now they gave short reports, tried to be civil if they were eating dinner together, and then retreated to their separate cocoons. She said, quickly, as if continuing a conversation, "So you'll have the house to yourself from the third through the sixth."

Bernard set down the bowl he'd been whisking something in. "You're really gonna do this."

Not again! "Of course. We need to reconnect." Could he, an only child, understand the dynamics here?

He turned. They were inches apart. "You always said it was a nasty town. Tijuana on the beach."

Easy, she cautioned herself, *you're gonna start hyperventilating.* "Anne thinks it's a positive thing."

"Uh-huh. Well, she's the professional. I'm just the husband." He yanked the oven door open. "And you never discussed it with me." He shoved a casserole in, slammed the door shut. "This'll take about an hour. I'm goin' for a run." He left.

Kathy went back to her studio and slumped down on the floor. Ever since he'd found out Leo had been chosen as the new department head, Bernard had been on a slow burn. More than once she'd heard him cursing at his book in the bedroom. But to take it out on her? *No.* She pulled her sketch pad down from the desk and stared at it, then threw it against the wall. From her vantage point on the floor, she could see all the dust bunnies she'd missed and one large dead cockroach.

Bernard ran lightly for a few blocks. *You're being an asshole*, he told himself. His right hip was talking to him, so he slowed to a fast walk. Raised his eyes to the familiar foothills, but no comfort there today.

Walking, he felt the neighborhood as he didn't when he ran through it. All these families, mostly whites, some Asians, a few Mexicans, their toys, bikes, cacti gardens, some MAGA signs here and there, no Black Lives Matter, of course. He had that old familiar feeling, like he was the only Black man in the Sonoran Desert. Unless you counted Leo. Which he didn't.

Kathy. Katharine Margaret Talley was driving him crazy. That furtive, panicky look she had always had when the subject of Rincón Bay came up, and now she was going there with her demented sister and her mentally ill half-dead brother?

Rarely had she even hinted at an explanation for her loathing of the Mexican beach town. Only a few times. Years ago at Becca's wedding reception, when he'd gone outside to escape the blare of the music and Kathy had had the same idea and he was just about to encircle her in a big tipsy hug, she looked at him with the goofy smile that meant she'd been drinking. But no, it was more like a grimace. Tears started streaming down her face. He remembered—why?—that she was wearing a tie-dyed dress she'd gotten for the occasion, and he thought she was as pretty as a layer cake and he wanted to eat her up, one bite at a time, but she was crying and, in a small voice, she said that Corina, also tipsy, of course, had suggested she should go on a diet.

"That beanpole?" Bernard responded.

Kathy just kept on blubbering and putting herself down, she was fat (she was not!) and she hated her freckles (they were adorable) and she was an awful person.

"You're *what*?" Bernard said. "You give blood, you volunteer at the Y with those immigrant classes, you do all kinds of stuff for people."

"But I left J on the beach!"

"What beach? We're in Sedona," he said, "the ocean's like a thousand miles away. And who's J?"

"I left J there in Rincón," she repeated, and when she stumbled back into the disco-playing party he let her go, because he didn't know what else to do.

The next day she was hungover and sullen when he asked her about who this Mexican J beach-person was. "Oh, I don't remember, it was nothing, I just had too many mojitos," she said.

Then, another time, maybe four, five years later, she woke him up screaming from a bad dream, yelling, "I didn't mean to! I didn't mean to!"

"What?" he mumbled, half-asleep, and she calmed down when he held her, and they both fell back asleep.

He did an easy run back to the townhouse. Kathy had gone to her cubbyhole. Maybe she was working on her art now; he hoped she was. He took out the casserole and started putting together the salad.

"Something smells good," Kathy said, emerging again. She smiled stiffly, the way she did when she was pissed off. She got trays and opened two beers. They sat and ate on the couch, watching the news, not talking.

After dinner, Bernard went to his desk and stared at the last chapter of *Music Without Walls*. Was he forcing the parallels between these two geniuses? Fucking Leo, gleefully planting his seeds of doubt. *But hold on*. He wrote at top speed:

Think about the variations of "Twinkle, Twinkle, Little Star'" in "Eine kleine Nachtmusik." A jazz essential, to play over a predetermined set of chord changes, and Wolfgang had understood that in 1787. Now Mozart, of course, often improvised straight to paper, but he also left space on the page for spontaneous creation, at a time when it had long been driven underground. And what about his Piano Concerto No. 26 with sections left blank in the piano part? *Left blank, for improvisation.* And, like Bird with Swing-era musicians, Wolfgang's peers thought his stuff was a mess. He went way over their heads: take "The Musical Joke"—not a joke! He used techniques that were innovative, decried, not understood at the time, but *they would be employed as a matter of course for more than two hundred years.* In the twentieth? There's an historic meeting between Charlie Parker—Bird—and Igor Stravinsky, at the eponymous club Birdland, a basement dive on 52nd Street that is a temple for jazz innovation. Stravinsky comes to hear the jazz saxophonist everyone keeps urging him to. Of course, Stravinsky is a huge celebrity, but not only to European classical fans: hip jazz fans love his Ebony Concerto, composed in 1946 for Woody Herman and his Orchestra. Stravinsky and his group are given a ringside table. Bird comes onto the tiny stage with his quartet and one of the musicians whispers to him, "Igor Stravinsky is in the house!" Bird shows no reaction but immediately calls his tune *Koko*, at a breakneck tempo and at the beginning of his second chorus, interpolates the opening of Stravinsky's *Firebird Suite* perfectly. At which, Stravinsky roars and pounds the table, sending the liquor and ice cubes in the glasses on it flying onto the next table. People duck and throw up their hands.

Wolf and Bird were trailblazers, soaring past existing musical conventions into new terroritory," Bernard concluded. "The young Beethoven idolized Mozart. And Stravinsky was blown away by Parker."

He read back what he'd written and chuckled. Instead of "territory," he'd typed "terror-itory." That too! The terrifying task that Bird, as a Black American man, had undertaken! The establishment dissed him, of course, all but a few. He didn't play smooth, he was a random muddler, a weirdo. But Bird, the preeminent progenitor of modern jazz, said, "There's no boundary line to art." You can hear Mozart calling out the amens from down the centuries.

Much of what he was writing might be discarded, but later for that. Wolf and Bird in the same ether, ethereal geniuses bound together . . . creating something *new*.

Bernard got up, peed, went to the living room. The TV was still on, low, but no Kathy. Nor was she in her study. Not on the patio.

What the fuck? He heaved a sigh, sank onto the couch, turned up the volume, and surfed for a show.

Kathy had gone to Mirabel's, where once again she sat on the patio of the restaurant, though this time alone at a corner table. She'd brought her sketch pad and pencils, not that she intended to draw, but as a kind of shield. She couldn't remember the last time she'd been out alone at night at a restaurant/bar. Surrounded by couples, groups, all of them giddy with life—no, wait, there was an unhappy pair across the way, the woman drooping over her plate, the man with a fixed glare. She was schadenfreudenly comforted by the duo.

The waitperson arrived and started reeling off the specials, but Kathy shook her head. "Just a drink. A vodka tonic, I think. Yeah."

Make that a double, she thought. A triple. A sea of vodka. She rarely drank hard alcohol anymore, but tonight it was an irresistibly appealing idea. And maybe a cigarette. Or a joint? *Oh, that's right, no smoking in public places anymore, how silly of me.*

Kathy snorted at herself. *Pull yourself together, you've had problems with him before. Who doesn't with their partner?* She rolled that word around mentally and found it wanting. "Partner" always reminded her of lawyers, which reminded her of divorce lawyers. She and Bernard had been together since the late 1980s, her entire adulthood, basically, and his. Marriage counseling once—six? No, seven years ago. After his affair with that grad student. The kids still at home. Probably why he agreed to go. For just three sessions. Wow, Bernard.

Her vodka tonic arrived. As she drank it, the time shortly after they'd started living together, when they went looking for cheap furniture, came into her mind, she wasn't sure why. Bernard was enthusing over a table at some antique store in Connecticut that was too pricey. But he had to have it. They lugged it back to their small apartment on Avenue B in a rental van the next weekend, where Bernard polished it to a silken gloss. She saw his bent head over his beloved table, the narrowed, concentrated planes of his face. And now it was in their bedroom against the bedroom window, covered with his laptop, books, yellow pads, the printer at one end. He spent more time with the table than he did with her. Working on the book.

That book. A *bloodsucker*. He claimed it was almost done, finally, the finale, the grand conclusion of his thoughts about music and giftedness and race. What would happen after he finished *Without Walls*? He was unhappy with the job, unhappy with that clown picked over him as head, unhappy with her. It felt as if everything was rushing to some foregone dreaded conclusion, like a bad dream. Bernard, she sensed, had come to the cliff edge of parsing, paralleling, and positing, and soon he would have no more to say *musicologically* but also, she feared, *maritally*.

She knew him so well. Knew he was wearing his life like a musty old coat. And suspected that he wanted a new one.

She ordered another vodka tonic. Finished it in short order. And again wished she had a cigarette, though she had quit twenty years ago. For longer than that, Bernard had been her rock, a man who seemed equal to the challenges life threw at him. He hadn't been tripped up—or not much—by the fault lines in America's race mythology. He was sturdy, solid. Yes, yes: all the things she would have liked in a father instead of that flickering image, disappearing into his den.

She didn't bother looking for Bernard when she got home. Instead, she went to the living room to watch TV.

Lying on the couch, she half watched some show about an improbably beautiful lawyer drawn into an even more improbable serial-killer scenario. She fell asleep just after the lawyer had been trussed and stuffed in a box in an abandoned warehouse, makeup intact, and she dreamed she was in her childhood bunk bed (the bottom, by seniority). Her mother was sitting beside her, pressing a cloth to her feverish forehead. Outside were the shrill sounds of the neighborhood kids playing, but she had no desire to be with them; for once she had her mother's full attention. The sun streaming through the white curtains at the window, a pastel gold.

She must have sensed something, a shadowy presence, and she opened her eyes, the dream vanishing. She sat up. "What?" she said loudly at Bernard.

"You were shouting. I thought something had happened."

"Shouting? But I was happy." She sat up and saw that his eyes were glistening.

"You yelled 'Mommy.' Several times."

"How embarrassing." Terribly thirsty—*Those vodka tonics*, she thought with a wince—she drained the half-full glass of water on the table.

"Well, you always say she was pretty distracted as a mother." He paused. "At least you had one."

Why was he bringing that up now? He hardly ever mentioned his mother, Louise "Lulu" Banks. Although in recent years, Lulu had sent Christmas and birthday cards to Bernard, no doubt out of some stubbornly long, lingering maternal guilt for abandoning him.

"Look," he said. "Can we—"

"I don't want to—" she said at the same time.

"About before," he went on. "I've been in a piss-poor mood. No excuse. But. Where were you? You disappeared on me."

"I just drove around." She rubbed her eyes and yawned. "Have you been working on the book all this time?"

"You smell of booze," he said, and walked away.

She sighed. *I thought vodka didn't leave an odor.*

CHAPTER 19

"**K**athy asked if we want to come with her to a Black Lives Matter demo tomorrow at one. I said I'd talk to you."

Toby set down the giant mug of latte he always started his day with. "You wanna go? Go." After he finished his coffee, all he wanted to do was lie in the hammock under the maple tree in his backyard. Where he could mope, as Becca called what he'd been doing lately, in private. But for Chrissake, he was mourning.

"It might get our minds off . . . you know."

"Are you fucking kidding me?" It had been eight days, a lifetime, since Cam had been taken away in the dead of night to that wilderness place and it was like it happened five minutes ago too. Toby hadn't slept through a single night since. He kept reliving the scene when Cam was hauled out of the house. Cam bellowing and cursing, Becca hiding on the top step of the stairs down to the cellar, Toby pacing in their bedroom with the door closed—okay, he was hiding too—while the two goons (licensed and insured) from the wilderness place rousted Cam, still drunk, out of bed at three in the morning. Cam shouting that he was gonna fucking run away the first chance he got from you fucking assholes. Banging and scuffling sounds, deep mumbles from the "escorts," the front door slamming, car doors, an engine starting and then—silence. He and Becca had crept into the living room and clung to each other, two broken dolls. Toby now knew what people meant when they said they "couldn't get over" something. He would never get over that night. Above all, his sense of having betrayed his son, never mind that it was supposed to be for his own good. He knew that. But he wasn't sure he believed it.

"We should go to the rally," Becca said.

That night when Cam was kidnapped, Becca eventually made tea. They sat in the living room letting it grow cold. At some point, he fetched some blankets and then he must have dozed off, because he jerked awake as Becca let out a howl. "What have we done? Toby, we have no idea where our boy is!"

Toby groggily checked his watch. "They should be on the connecting flight now, if all has gone well." Gone well! He buried his face in his hands. "The worst night of my life!"

"Both of our lives," Becca corrected him.

Now, a little over a week later, she stared at him, waiting.

What difference did it make? Wherever he was, he would do nothing but focus on his personal nightmare.

"Yeah, okay, I'll go to the rally," he said.

Pete had fully intended to unload the old Buick this time, but somehow it was still in the parking lot of the apartment complex. But he had vowed not to drive it anymore, so he called a taxi for his dialysis appointment (which, oddly, he'd learned, Medicaid would actually pay for) and he enjoyed sparring so much with his redneck driver about the corny country music he played on the way there that he made a deal with him—guy's name was Buck, for Pete's sake—to be his regular driver.

Emerging from the four-hour session of clearing out his kidneys, he was pleasantly surprised not to feel as wiped out as usual, plus the cramps in his legs were minimal. He told Buck to go by the park on the way to the apartment and stop there for a minute. He wanted to check out the Black Lives Matter action.

"There's a bunch of pinkos there protesting for the coloreds," Buck demurred.

"Pinkos! Coloreds!" Pete echoed, delightedly appalled. "Yeah, my sisters are there, I might run into them. Plus, my sister's *colored* husband. Are you gonna take me there or not?"

"It's your funeral. But I'm not stickin' around." Buck drove, a sour vibe now twanging between them. Arriving at the park, he cruised slowly down the street. "Now what? 'Cause, like I said, I'm not stoppin.'"

"I'm the customer, so I say stop."

"Hell, no. You want me to stop, you leave."

"Oh? You gonna kick a sick man to the curb? Way to go, Buck. Buck, what kinda redneck racist name is that anyway?"

The cabbie turned around, glaring at him. "Out. And let's hope some Proud Boys came here. They'll show you all what's what."

Pete shook his head and inched himself out of the car. "Asshole, I'm not payin' you a cent after that remark."

"Eight dollars!"

Pete snorted. "Put it on my tab." He was wobbly but psyched. "By the way," he said, "this is what I think of you and your politics." He lifted both his middle fingers.

Buck roared off as Pete remained standing with his middle fingers in the air. He then made his slow way across the street to the park. "What's going down?" he asked a white kid with a BLM baseball cap.

The kid sized him up. Pete knew what he saw: a tall, skinny older guy with tape on his glasses and stubble on his chin, wearing an off-white T-shirt and a baggy, greasy pair of jeans. *Probably thinks I'm homeless.*

"This probably isn't the best scene for you, old man." The kid tilted his head, scanned him again. "Need some food? I gotta extra granola bar."

"Food?" Pete exclaimed. "No."

A roar arose from inside the park. "Cool." The kid turned, clearly itching to get to the action.

Pete didn't need food but did, he realized, need wheels. "Hey, can I use your cell phone? To call a cab?"

The kid hesitated. "Uh, sure."

Now they heard yelling and a few screams. Some people came running in their direction.

"What the fuck?" said the kid.

"What's the address here?"

"Oh man, I don't know." The kid found it on his phone. "Here, I'll do it."

"Any cab company will do."

The kid worked the phone nervously, talked to a dispatcher. He dropped the hand holding the phone to his side, looked at Pete. "It's on its way. Mannie's, it's called."

There was a loud report like gunfire. More screams. The kid ran off and Pete moved back into the street, dazed at the sight of all the people running by.

"Like the old days all over again," he said to no one. "Groundhog Day." He felt exhilarated, then strange. Everything started to sway and flicker. He felt very tall and light. "Ah, shit," he said as he fell.

Kathy, Becca, and Toby were in the crowd streaming from the park. It had started as a good old-fashioned demo, heartfelt little speeches by people who passed a hand mic around. Some MAGA hats and Orangeman T-shirts were milling around the edges, the rumor went, but before anything could develop there was the cracking sound of what everybody assumed was a gun, and it sent them flying. Though for once it was just a car backfiring.

Becca stopped at the curb. "Whoa. Isn't that Pete?"

"Jesus." Kathy's eyes widened. "It is. Pete!"

Nobody had stopped for the scruffy homeless-looking guy lying right in front of them.

"Assholes!" screamed Kathy.

Pete was conscious, but he'd cut his arm when he fell and it was bleeding. Kathy checked his head. No apparent injuries there. Toby got him to his feet and helped him shuffle to Becca's car. There was a cloth in the trunk, not quite clean but all they had to wrap around his arm.

They took him to an urgent care nearby.

A nurse at the urgent care treated Pete's cut and advised him to go to the hospital.

"It's just a cut," Pete protested. Naturally, he loathed hospitals. The cramped rooms with dying roommates, the hassled nurses, the smells, the food, the stupid gowns that opened at the back, the probing and tubing and, most of all, the rare cameos of the poker-faced doctors. He loathed above all the female doc with the mustache who had told him in a thick accent that it was his fault he was in there because he was an addict. He imagined the complaint he'd file with HR: "Dr. Abershnatzi has a bad attitude and she speaks lousy English."

"You fell," a nurse said after the doctor whirled out of the compartment. "You might have a concussion."

"I'm fine. Just need to eat somethin.'"

The nurse sighed and gave him a packet of crackers and a bottle of water. "Dialysis patients can be tricky," she said, turning to his hovering family. "Someone needs to keep an eye on him for the next twenty-four hours. It's very important. If he falls asleep, wake him up every couple of hours. If he won't wake up, call 911 immediately." She shook her head and went to the next bed to attend to a distraught mother's squalling baby.

"Shit," said Toby.

"Yeah, that about sums it up. Shall we take it in shifts? Like, twenty-four divided by three?" suggested Kathy.

"Shit," said Toby again.

"You can have the first one," Becca said to him. "Watch a game. Or three. Like you would anyway if you were home?"

Pete saw Becca cock her head at her husband. Like, *I dare you to say no.*

Kathy, arriving for the last shift, made coffee and scrambled eggs and toast for breakfast. Pete was sitting in the Barcalounger, looking like his new-normal self. Not good, but no worse than usual.

She carried a tray the several steps to the tiny living room. "You're up. How did you sleep?" She already knew from Becca, who had whispered "Freedom!" to her when she left, that their brother had not been a cooperative patient.

"Oh great, somebody slapping my face every few minutes and yelling, 'Wake up!' Just peachy, as Mom used to say."

"But you don't have a headache, dizziness, anything like that?"

"Nada."

"Oh, Pete, maybe it's not a good idea to go to Rincón right now."

"Nah, I wanna get some fishing in, snorkeling, the whole nine yards. I'm good, I tell you."

"Oh, Pete."

CHAPTER 20

Toby stared at the mess on his desk—the papers, Post-it Notes, books in sliding piles—then at the screen of his laptop, blank, mocking him, as if he had nothing more to say about . . . anything. On the wall above him to the right was the framed Deems Taylor award for his *John Prine: Proust of the Midwest*. Twelve long years ago, an idyllic-seeming time now (he tended to forget the bedlam of Cam's hitting and biting toddlerhood). On the strength of the book, Toby had been offered, with a little help from Bernard, a two-year contract at the U of A. He and Becca, hoping the contract would lead to a regular job, threw a party. Becca planned to scale back her hours managing the craft shop and work more on her poetry. She'd been singled out as promising in college, did the workshops and had a chapbook, *Missed Intentions*, in the works. But money always got in the way. They were still in the starter house, with the little backyard (which Ward and Julia had given them the down payment for). They'd hoped to be able to move once the nibbles of interest about a biopic of Prine turned into a movie deal.

But the Prine project had died on the vine and, somehow, none of his other TV or streaming projects panned out. "The market's changing," his agent had unhelpfully pointed out. Toby had cobbled together teaching gigs, two classes at the community college and two sections at the U of A on a perennial favorite, "Pop and Drop: The Music and Mores of American Popular Music, 1955 to 1975." The head of the music department then was an old fossil who idolized Wagner even though the head was (also) Jewish, which in Toby's opinion was nonsensical. Hitler had idolized Wagner, for Chrissake.

Somehow, Becca never could manage to work fewer hours, though she did get raises. Then came Cam's troubles—the fights and talking back to teachers, the vodka bottle found in his locker, tanking grades, and the outlays for tutoring and therapy.

Yet there were happy times too. Hiking together, digging the small but thriving arts scene in Tucson, the more interesting inexpensive restaurants.

There was nothing in particular, no one moment that Toby could pinpoint when life became a chore. Becca's long hours, her lack of time to do the work she loved and be with Cam, Toby's more flexible schedule, making him the at-home parent who drove Cam around, oversaw as best he could that homework got completed. He'd thought he was doing a good job. He loved being a father, most of the time, considered himself to be laid-back and empathetic. When he discovered Cam was smoking weed in his room—the rolled-up towel under the door didn't block the smell—he cut Cam some slack: Wasn't getting high a universal teenage rite of passage? When Cam got in trouble at school, he felt that the teachers needed to lighten up.

He'd gotten it wrong.

They'd all trudged along. Summers were the worst. Too hot to be outside, but they couldn't afford more than a week away. The little adobe house needed a lot of upkeep. Toby tried to keep up with his writing projects, but he was distracted by his struggles, money problems, rejections, Cam. Becca snapped at him more and more. He needed to get a job, she said, one with a steady paycheck instead of the irregular adjunct and freelance-writer income. Toby told her he didn't want to turn into one of those old duffers who helped women find stuff at Home Depot or at the checkout line. She said, "Well, what's wrong with that? Just till one of your projects comes through." She hadn't written any poetry that he knew of for a while.

The night Cam came home drunk after he'd failed to help Phil fix his damaged wall and again went into a rage when Becca confronted him, striking her on the cheek, was when Toby had given up and let Becca call the rehab.

So here he was, dried-up at his computer, his boy somewhere in the wilds of Idaho, learning how to man up.

And Toby's new job, twenty hours a week at a True Value Hardware store, started next week.

PART TWO

CHAPTER 21

Becca was annoyed, though for once not at Toby. She had already been upset when she learned that she would have to make the long drive alone down to Rincón Bay in the Mini Cooper. All because of a sudden stupid conference call about some mandatory new gender-fluidity training at work that she'd forgotten was scheduled for Friday afternoon, right when the rest of her sibs planned to take off for the beach. And then, worse, it had gone even later than expected. By the time she was finally free to throw together a sandwich and make sure she had a flashlight, extra batteries, bug spray, and a sweater—the desert could be chilly at night—and throw her suitcase in the back seat, she was almost two hours behind schedule.

On her way out, she stopped at Toby's little study.

"I'm leaving now."

He frowned. "Isn't it a bit late? I don't like the thought of you driving in Mexico at night."

She shrugged. "I've driven that road at least four times."

"Not on your own."

"I'll be fine."

He looked so hapless, she had to give him a hug. He hugged her back, a bit awkwardly.

"Call me when you get there."

"Of course."

When Becca was gone, Toby felt... How did he feel? Abandoned? Free? Free to worry about Cam up in Idaho, free to worry about the cost of it—about a year at an Ivy League school. Free to worry about the second mortgage they'd gotten on the house, just avoiding another dip into their modest 401(k).

Toby sighed. When he thought of the western wilderness, he thought of angry mother bears, wolves, trampling herds of buffalo. What was Cam doing there? Fishing? Chopping wood? Cleaning latrines? Did he speak up in group therapy? He must be scared, if for no other reason than he was bongless. Cam's bong had been attached to his hip.

How the fuck did we get here? Toby wondered again. He buried his face in his hands. *Pull yourself together, man. Focus. Finish the pitch, order a pizza, watch something online. Or maybe take a bike ride. Or call Marc or Bernard, go out and live dangerously at the Freakness.*

But first he stretched out on the couch, the cat warming his legs. He intended to nap for a bit, but that turned into four hours, during which he didn't hear his cell phone repeatedly ringing.

Becca had been rolling along. She'd managed to avoid all but the tail end of rush hour and was now nearing Highway 8 in Mexico, sixty miles of bleak two-lane driving to the bay.

She practically zipped past the border—always easier on the way in than the way out—after which the mediocre American highway became noticeably worse. She ate trail mix and a banana, drank her water.

As she drove, Becca tried not to think about Cam. *Think about this vacation, our mini family reunion*, she told herself. But that made her think about the family vacation they'd planned for August, she and Toby and Cam, to Cabo. They'd been there several times, rented a tiny condo that was cheaper because it was in town, not on the beach. Toby and Cam always went out on a fishing boat at least once, and they had their favorite little places for meals.

Don't think about that! she yelled in her head. *Don't think about him! Think about lying in a beach chair under an umbrella with a mojito and a paperback. With the sibs. Think about the poems you might write, those baby birds chirping in your brain. Three days of not thinking about Cam. You can do this.*

The sun was lowering as she breezed along on the nearly empty road. Suddenly the Mini Cooper rolled to a stop.

"Shit?"

Becca looked at the gas gauge. For the first time.

"Shit! You idiot! Shit, shit!" She who was so well-organized. She who did not forget things. She who had forgotten the most basic thing: to gas up the car. She grabbed her phone. Well, that's what AAA was for.

No service.

The rest of the Talleys, piled into Kathy's car, were even later starting off for Rincón Bay. *I should have remembered*, Kathy thought. *All the drama.*

Corina had not finished packing when Kathy and Pete arrived, or rather, she had not allowed Imalia to finish. Pete lured Corina out of the bedroom on some excuse and Kathy and Imalia quickly completed the job. Next time they went anywhere, if there was a next time, Kathy vowed she'd hide Corina's prepacked bag.

Next, Corina, the sushi queen who had to be coaxed to eat at every meal, announced she was hungry and insisted on having scrambled eggs, bacon, and whole wheat toast. So everyone sat around while Imalia cooked and Corina picked at her food.

When they finally got going, it was almost midafternoon. And Kathy's Outback was crammed, as full as it could possibly be, with four people and their bags, including a ridiculous three for Corina. After those got shoved in, Kathy slid into the driver's seat with Pete beside her, his long legs hanging awkwardly over the cooler with water bottles on the floor of the car, Corina and Imalia in the back, the middle seat taken up with stuff. How had they thought they could possibly have fit all five of them? Good thing Becca had called to say she'd have to drive down on her own.

Once on the highway, traffic was a crawl. A fire truck blared past on the shoulder. Kathy pummeled the steering wheel. If Corina hadn't insisted on the breakfast of her childhood and then getting out of the car once they were ready to go, running off to look for the blasted tortoise one more time (of course he was hiding: they'd searched all the bushes before Imalia finally found him under a rock in the remotest part of the garden), they would have missed rush hour. Oh, and if Corina's cell phone hadn't disappeared (Imalia found that too, under a towel in the bathroom) and Pete hadn't had to use the bathroom again, and then it was time for his meds, a complex cornucopia.

"Shall we put on one of your CDs?" she asked Corina now as evenly as she could manage. Corina had insisted on bringing along several.

No answer.

"Well, I'll take that for a yes."

They'd gotten through almost all of *Sergio Mendes & Brasil '66's Greatest Hits* before traffic started moving slowly again in the metal-burning, fume-spewing heat.

"I have this book," Corina said, rummaging in her bag and holding it up.

"What is it?" Kathy and Pete replied in unison.

"About, you know, what I have. I'm in the middle stage now."

Silence. No one was about to contradict her, but that ship had sailed.

What can you say? Kathy wondered. *I'm sorry you have dementia and are still occasionally rational enough to know it?* "You know what?" she said. "Let's just forget everything but having fun. Just relax, talk about the good stuff." *What BS,* she thought immediately, and she turned, briefly, looking at the endless desert to hide the tears that sprang up.

And as soon as she did, an electric thread of dread jolted through her: an image of a girl in a torn and bloody cotton dress bordered with flowers running on sand. *No,* she told herself, *not now.* She remembered tips Anne had given her to de-stress. *Think about where your feet are. That's it, keep your eyes on the road, feel your hands competently on the wheel.*

She took several deep breaths. *I'm going to be with my family.*

Corina held up her other CDs and slowly named them: Buckwheat Zydeco, Professor Longhair, Creedence Clearwater, Joe Cocker, Bill Frisell, and some Mozart concertos. (Kathy pushed away the thought of Bernard.) The sibs argued lightheartedly about what to play next. They let Pete win and sang along to "Born on the Bayou," even Pete (though not Imalia, of course, but she was *giggling*). Pete passed around water bottles from the cooler. He was air-guitaring and Corina was laughing. And they were moving, slowly but surely, south.

Kathy smiled and then yawned, suddenly tired. She hadn't slept well since . . . *Well, don't go there either.* But it was good, the three of them together like this. And in a few hours, Becca would complete their foursome.

The last song on the album faded out.

"Imalia?" Kathy said after the lengthy silence that followed, glancing in the rearview mirror.

"*Sí?*" Imalia raised her drooping head.

"Did I wake you? The thing is, I'm sleepy too. I wonder, would you mind driving for maybe an hour?" Who else could she ask? Pete? She wasn't going there. Imalia had a car; she'd had driving lessons. "*Por favor? Puedes manejar por un rato? Porque necesito descansar.*"

Their eyes met in the rearview mirror. Nope. Terror there. Okay then, she'd have to stop at the next plausible place to rest a bit. If there was one. She didn't remember. Did it even matter what time they got to Rincón Bay? *Nope, it's the journey, not the desti*—Kathy, yawning hugely, spotted a Burger King on a ridge on the right. She took the exit.

"Pit stop and food," she announced.

"*Burger King?*" Corina screwed up her face. "Ew."

"Corina, do you see any other choices? And I badly need some coffee."

"I'm sure it's crap coffee."

"If it has caffeine in it, that's all I care about." *Snippy, snippy,* she thought, rolling her eyes. And really, what was Corina on about? The Corina who'd demanded rare, high-end coffee beans and the costliest machine on the market to brew it in no longer existed, as far as she was concerned.

Pete opened the door on his side. "I need to use the can."

"Then I'll come too," said Corina. As if she had a choice.

Imalia sat there.

"Imalia, you can't stay in the car. You'll roast to death!" Corina told her.

They piled out into the furnace of the slowly dying desert day and shuffled into Burger King, where, true to form, a pasty-faced blonde with pink-tipped hair lounged behind the counter, a small Latinx guy mopped the floor, and the tables and booths were empty except for an ancient white couple who seemed to be content to stare at their burgers, fries, and Cokes. Corina clutched Kathy's arm, Pete shuffled off to the bathroom, and Imalia trailed behind.

Kathy pointed to a booth overlooking the parking lot. "Will this do, Princess C.?" They slid in. "Oh wait, it's self-serve. What do you guys want?"

"What is this place again?"

"Burger King. Do you want something to eat?"

"Maybe."

"Imalia?"

Imalia looked longingly at the parking lot.

Pete sat down. "Hey, I'm hungry."

Kathy said, "Just coffee, Pete. It's not renal-friendly here."

Pete snorted. "One burger's not gonna hurt."

"We have approved snacks in the car. I'll just get us some coffees if nobody's gonna order anything."

She didn't wait for Pete to argue back; she slid out of the booth and went straight to the counter. In under two minutes, she was back with five coffees in a cardboard carrier.

"Here you go," she said as she set them down on the table. "There's plenty of milk."

"I have to have it black," Pete informed them. "I'm lactose intolerant now. I'm everything intolerant."

"Well, I'm *nothing*," Corina said.

"Well, this is not fun," Kathy said in a fake-jolly voice that she immediately despised herself for. "Guys, come on, we're on vacation."

Imalia put three sugar packets in her coffee and three milks. Her phone, sitting in front of her on the table, began to buzz.

"Do you need to get that?" Kathy asked.

Imalia darted a look at Corina, then said, "Yes. Excuse me." She stood, phone in hand, and beelined for the bathroom.

In a stall, Imalia put the seat down and, somewhat miraculously she thought, the callback went through.

"Hi, *corazon*, I miss you. Yeah, it's weird but they're paying me a lot so . . . What? No! I won't get into *trouble* there, mi amor. Norita, it's families down there." She giggled. "Yeah, some moms are hot. But not as hot as you. And by the way, don't flirt with anybody at Lola's—don't even smile! Okay, I gotta go take care of the *locos*. I'll call you tomorrow. No, *you* be good, amor. Kiss, kiss."

Back at the table, waiting for her, they all got up.

"Where have you been, Imalia?" Señora Corina asked. "I thought you'd gone somewhere."

"She went to the bathroom," Señora Kathy said briskly. "Come on, let's get going."

"Were you talking to your girlfriend?" Señora Corina continued. "You were, weren't you?"

Imalia was mute. Señora Corina was *loca como una zorra*. Crazy like a fox.

Straining to help Pete get out of the booth, Señora Kathy said, "Shall we change the subject, Corina?"

"They talk all the time at my house," Señora Corina persisted.

"Will you give it a rest?" Señora Kathy grasped her sister's arm quite firmly as they headed for the car. Señor Pete toddled along, Imalia again bringing up the rear.

Imalia was embarrassed but defiant. So they all knew now. It was none of their business, but she found she didn't really care that they knew. She had learned a lot since coming to Arizona, especially since learning to drive. Having a car had led her like a laser to Lola's, the LGBTQIA+ bar in her neighborhood. This was who she was—a *lencha*, a woman who loved women.

Imalia dozed off in her corner of the chilly yet hot car as it pursued its flat way into her homeland and to the ocean that she had never seen before.

The one-lane traffic moved at a crawl again. *Just my luck, an accident*, Kathy thought. She wanted to get there; she wanted to get it over with. It. *Chill*, she told herself, and she put on one of her own CDs, flamenco guitar, low. *I've got to steer the ship. I am in charge. I have to do this.* Though the land was flat, she had the sense that they were slowly rolling downhill. Around the car the superheated air still shimmered, but the sun was lower now and soon it would be dark.

Her thoughts drifted to her children. Tamara, her coffee-with-loads-of-cream complexion, freckles, long black curls, a sweet baby, a sullen teenaged beanpole. The memorable year they lived in South Africa when Bernard taught at the University of Cape Town, Tamara had had a major meltdown when she came home from school the first day to the apartment they'd rented. She announced that everybody said she was colored. Not Black, colored. Bernard had explained the South African caste system when he got home. Kathy remembered how Tamara cut her off when she started adding her take. "Mom! *You* don't get it." Theo had turned twelve that year, always off playing soccer, a sturdy brown child who couldn't care less about racial nomenclature, fitting right in with his fast dribbling and bodychecking skills. Now that Tamara was in her midtwenties, she was close to Kathy again; well, closer. Even if race was a construct, a concept, a *fabrication* really, down-on-the-ground people had to deal with it—people of color, as Tamara now called herself. Kathy thought about the Tamara who had come home for spring break, tall and lovely and smart and cynical. Still had those freckles but she had cut her hair so that tight waves nestled next to her scalp. *Your children grow up, but you never lose your hunger for their touch,* she thought. *And the more you long for it, the more they pull away.* Tamara was not physical with her; for that Kathy had her boy. Theo usually came by for Sunday dinner, sometimes with his current boyfriend. Would watch a game with Dad when he was solo.

Why are you so pissed at me? Now she was thinking of Bernard. Moodier, wary even at times, irritatedly shutting the door to the bedroom/study. Recently, when he was barricaded at his desk as usual these days, she had to go in because she needed to change for work; she couldn't wear the baggy white shorts and T-shirt she habitually wore around the house. He'd turned around and, for a moment, it was as if she were a stranger. There'd been a flat look in his eyes.

"You're obsessed," she mentally told Bernard.

"Obsessed? Who, me? About what?" Pete asked, slightly slurring his words, from sleepiness or oxies.

Kathy shot him a glance. "Geez, was I talking out loud? I didn't realize. That wasn't about you."

"Yeah, well," said Pete, "I *am* obsessed with getting off this road. Can you stop for a minute? I need to stretch my legs and, you know, relieve myself."

The sky was indigo now; the stars were coming out. It was taking forever to get to Rincón. But it was a welcome several degrees cooler. As she slowed down and indicated she was pulling off the road, Kathy had that fleeting image of a woman running in the ruined cotton dress again. Then it was gone. Her hands trembled at the wheel.

"Pit stop," she said, rolling carefully to the side. "Last stop before the bay."

Pete got out of the car.

"Don't wander into the scrub," she told him. "You never know what lurks in there."

"Yes, Mother."

Kathy did some breathing exercises to calm down. It was bound to happen, that shards of that night would intrude into her consciousness now that she was getting close. *The scene of the crime*, she thought. She got out of the car and stretched, watched Pete wander behind a saguaro, presumably to pee. Wobbling along like an old man. What the drugs and booze had done to him; or what he'd done to himself? People *get* cancer, Alzheimer's, Parkinson's. Hadn't Pete caused his own addiction? Okay, he hadn't chosen it, but he'd had many chances to stop.

"Hey!" Pete said, after shuffling back, "There's a car stopped just ahead."

She squinted. "Yeah, you're right. Pit-stop central, I guess."

"Should we go over there, see if, you know, everything's all right?"

"It's probably abandoned. Or full of desperados."

Pete guffawed. "Desperados," he drawled. "That's a good one."

"Cartel members, that better? But we'll check it out when we drive by. With the windows up."

In the stalled car, after she finished yelling, Becca had a short debate with herself: she might get attacked if she opened the windows, but if she left them up, she would eventually roast to death. But there was no way to roll them down without juice to the car. She cracked her door open. And oh God, now she had to pee.

She waited while some cars whizzed by. When the road seemed temporarily empty, she got out and squatted out of sight on the passenger side, thinking now of the creepy and venomous creatures that were active in the night. Snakes, spiders, scorpions. Rabid coyotes... She considered throwing her used tissues into the desert, but that was definitely bad karma, and she didn't need any more of that, so she stuffed them into the side pocket of the car door, then climbed into the back and lay down. Could things get any worse? *You know the answer to that*, came the faint reply.

At first there was mainly silence but for the whoosh of an occasional passing car; then she became attuned to the night music of timid chirps, skitters, hoots, flurries of wind. She thought about her son. No one but Toby knew the whole story of what had led them to send Cam to the wilderness camp in Idaho. His angry outbursts, his thoughtless risk-taking, she had told others about, mainly Kathy. Not that last time, when he lunged at her. And struck her. She was afraid of him now. But Becca felt only the poisonous guilt of a mother who has betrayed her child. She could not take it in.

Incredibly, she must have fallen asleep on the back seat because suddenly she was struggling to consciousness and there were shapes looming outside the car. Becca grabbed her vial of pepper spray (she had remembered that, if not the gas) and aimed.

Yells, curses.

"Are you okay?"

"It burns like hell!"

"I think I'm gonna puke!"

"Kathy, where are you? *Kathy!*" That was *Corina*'s voice.

"Pete? Oh shit, he's fallen!" And that was Kathy yelling!

"*You* guys?" Becca dropped the can. It rolled under the front seat.

"Kathy? It's me, Becca!"

Coughing and sputtering, Kathy leaned in the front window. "I know! We recognized your car!"

CHAPTER 22

Bernard looked at his watch. He had been staring at his laptop for over twenty minutes without writing a word. He got up. Maybe he'd go to his office on campus and do some paperwork for next semester, then grab a beer at the Freakness. Or a movie? Or wait, come back and stream *Bird* again, watch the young Forest Whitaker wrestle with the gargantuan role of playing Charlie Parker. Anything but work on the book.

But he ended up going for a run. As he jogged in the dusk, he stumbled and his ankle twisted.

Cursing violently, he cautiously tested it. He was all right, at least physically. Stuck in his ear-pod—*but nah, nah, don't go there*. No Bobby Womack exuberantly rolling over the pain of The End. He switched up the tune and shit, now it's B.B. King roaring like a lion with his glad-mad guitar about the same damn thing. Over, done, that's it. Like they were reading his mind.

Bernard ripped out the pod, but he could still hear a tiny, tinny B. B. lamenting.

I have got to stop this, Bernard thought, running flat out on the stretch of road all but empty of houses close to the foothills. He wasn't sure what he meant.

"What are the odds?" Becca had gotten out of the car and was handing out water bottles to Pete and Kathy and Corina to douse their heads against the pepper spray. "I am so sorry," she said again. She handed Kathy a box of tissues.

"Synchronicity," Kathy suggested between lessening gasps.

"I fell asleep, and I thought you were, you know, criminals," she said sheepishly. "I ran out of gas," she added.

"What the fuck, Bec?"

"I know, I *know*. Beyond stupid. But—how are you here now? I mean, you were leaving Tucson right after lunch."

"A long, long story," Kathy said tightly. "But a happy ending." She hugged Becca.

Imalia came up with beach towels she'd unearthed from the luggage, and they all toweled down.

"Well, that's better," Kathy said. "Look, we can't just stand around out here. We'll figure out about your car when we get there."

"But I can't just leave it here!" Her dear old Mini Cooper. No doubt stripped for parts before a tow truck could get here. And did their car insurance even cover Mexico?

"We need to get to town." Kathy lowered her voice. "Pete and Corina. Fried."

They turned as one to see their sister leaning against Imalia and weeping softly. Pete was already in the passenger seat, head back, eyes closed.

"Right. But how?"

Kathy and Becca removed the bags from the floor and seat in the back. Imalia, Corina, and Becca got in, Rubik's-Cubing the things that had fit when there was an empty seat, now stuffed onto laps, wedged under feet. Silently, they set off again.

They were closer to the bay than Kathy had thought. Soon the welcome sight of lights and the curve of the bay appeared. Except for the bay itself, Kathy doubted if she would recognize the place, the new sprawl of shops, hostels, the march of shanties behind and further on, the new hotels near the cliffs, where there had been nothing but scrub when she was nineteen. *Don't think about that.*

Now they had to find the Posada Carlota.

"In two miles, turn left at Avenida Plexiglasa," Becca said to Kathy, obedient to the distorted voice on her phone.

"Plexiglasa? That can't be a street name. Siri's illiterate in Spanish!"

"I'll watch the street signs," Becca assured her. Plexiglasa turned out to be Pedregosa Avenue. They went down several blocks and pulled up at what Siri said, this time correctly, was the Posada Carlota.

"This is our hotel?" Becca said doubtfully.

"It didn't look like *this* on the website." Kathy felt like screaming. On the internet, the posada was very slightly shabby chic. But in fact, in the flesh, it was totally shabby without the chic. "The reviews were good too," she added.

There was silence as they contemplated the stained low stucco walls, the construction debris mounded in front in lieu of landscaping, and the flickering sign: OSADA C RLOTA.

"My God, it's so—noir! Like something out of a Raymond Chandler movie," Becca exclaimed.

"Becca," Kathy replied in the same warning tone she'd used when Becca was an annoying child. "It's late, we're tired and hungry, let's just go in. Maybe it won't be too bad for one night?" She paused, sighed. "Pete, we're here. Pete." She shook his arm. He was *out*.

"*What?*" he roared as he came to with a start.

"We're at the hotel."

"Oh." He grappled violently with his seat belt. "I can't *deal* with this thing."

Corina said, "Is this a cantina? I'll have a margarita."

Kathy swallowed. "We'll go somewhere else tomorrow if it's, um, unsatisfactory inside."

Insisting on carrying his own bag, Pete staggered to the entrance. Imalia, Kathy, and Becca divided Corina's bags to carry along with their own.

They entered a tiny lobby with an empty fish tank. Kathy had a protracted conversation in Spanish with the young woman at the desk in which she tried to be firm yet diplomatic about the gulf between what the Posada Carlota advertised itself as and the reality. The receptionist pretended not to understand Kathy but was checked by Imalia. No matter, the manager was not on site nor reachable by phone.

Naturally, Kathy thought.

A porter who looked to be about twelve stacked everything on a cart and they followed him down a short hall to their rooms. Though small and viewless, they were, at least, clean. Kathy breathed a sigh of relief. They could stay the night and she'd hassle with the manager in the morning about a refund for the two remaining nights, which she'd—stupidly—paid for in advance.

The receptionist had confirmed they served dinner on the patio, so Kathy rounded up Pete and Becca got Corina and they both persuaded Imalia to come. The patio, dotted with a few tables and chairs, was otherwise deserted. In fact, the entire Posada Carlota seemed deserted. "What happened to the view?" Corina asked when they slid, exhausted, into their chairs. The table overlooked a parking lot. And no one came to serve them.

Kathy and Becca went back to reception and demanded, as nicely as they could, some service. Shortly after returning to the table, a young man appeared, who said they were closed.

"At eight o'clock? That's ridiculous. We're going to order," Becca told him.

Kathy translated, wheedling until he agreed to prepare some tacos.

"And guac?" Becca asked.

No guac.

"I want enchiladas suizas," Pete declared, "and a Corona."

Kathy felt as if a volcano had replaced her insides, molten lava and flames ready to erupt like a scene from *Rosemary's Baby*. "Listen," she said carefully, "we're getting whatever's in the tacos. I had to fight tooth and nail for them. The kitchen's closed, probably because nobody eats here. Or stays here. Except us. And no beer," she added.

"What the fuck?" Pete demanded.

"You don't drink beer anymore," Becca reminded him.

"I screwed up, okay?" Kathy shouted. "Mea culpa."

"We can switch hotels tomorrow," Becca soothed. "It's not that bad. One night, guys."

"This is the kind of dump college kids stay at on spring break," Corina commented.

Kathy winced. Actually, the Posada Carlota was probably better than that hostel she'd stayed at on spring break thirty years ago. *At least this place is clean.*

To their surprise, the tacos were not bad, served with cold drinks. Everyone was in a better mood by the time they shuffled off to their beds.

Kathy, eyes already half-closed, couldn't wait to collapse.

But peace and quiet were not to be. After she crawled into bed, Kathy lay staring at a water stain on the ceiling, her mind a series of flickering images of her nineteen-year-old self. Here in Rincón Bay at the bonfire on the beach. The loud music. Dire Straits? Running up the beach after too many margaritas with J staggering along beside her... The sky had been a bowl of hazy stars... Cut to a key gripped in her hand... Her heart thudded as she slipped into a dreamless sleep.

If the Posada Carlota had been more upscale, the walls would have been thicker, and Pete, whose room was next to Corina's, would not have heard anything. As it was, he heard loud thuds and yelling.

His first thought was that Corina was being attacked. He charged out in his boxers and T-shirt and pounded on her door.

Silence now.

"Corina?"

When she didn't respond, he ran to the lobby. No one there. He ran back and pounded on the door again.

"It's Pete. Open up, it's Pete!"

Suddenly, the door crashed open. Corina stared at him, doe-eyed and trembling.

"I couldn't get my bag open. I was so mad. I had to slam it on the floor. It finally worked. Where am I?"

Pete went inside. Stuff was strewn around. He removed some from the one chair and sat down, breathing heavily. "We're at a hotel. On vacation. You scared the shit out of me. I thought you were . . . I don't know, something bad."

She cocked her head, birdlike. "Oh." It came out as a long sigh. She threw out her arms. "What's wrong with me, Pete?"

"You get confused. Don't worry about it. You're okay, uh, we're all here together so . . . Hey, do you have some water? I'm really, really thirsty."

"Yes." She went in the bathroom. He heard the tap running. "No, no! We can't drink the tap water here."

Like flipping a light switch, Corina's old self reappeared, or something close to her old self. She nodded her head. "Montezuma's revenge. You certainly want to avoid that, Pete, you know, in your condition. Here, here's a bottle. I always bring a bunch with me." On the edge of her bed, she watched him drink avidly. The light switched off. "What are you doing in my room?"

"You know. I heard noise. You were yelling. I thought . . ."

"I was? I wonder why? Oh, because of . . . yep. It." She nodded and tapped her head. "Sorry about that."

"I'm just relieved you're okay."

"You polished off that water fast! Want another one?"

"No. No." Pete leaned back, uncomfortable. The water, along with the tacos he'd eaten, pushed like a fist against his stomach. "I don't feel so great."

"Oh, Pete, what's wrong?"

"My belly. They took out about two liters of fluid last time." He thought of the procedure. Paracentesis, a fancy word for sticking a needle in your belly and sucking out excess fluid. He had to have it done more and more often now.

"Aren't we a pair. The human condition at its most dire. Falling apart organ by organ," Corina said with cheerful detachment.

Pete winced. As usual when the topic got around to mortality, he had nothing to say.

"You've always been a mystery to me," she continued in a confidential tone. "Well, to the whole family."

"I know," he muttered.

"How did you get to *this*?"

He considered her. She was gaunt, but in a different way from him. Her face was puckered, drawn, her stick arms folded on her nonexistent lap. Yes, you *can* be too thin. Poor kid. She had lost her stylish-model look, that hair with the blonde streaks, the careful makeup. And all those clothes. Now she just wore baggy long-sleeved tops and shorts. Of the two of them, he thought she probably had the worst of it. Losing your mind, literally!

He said, "You know why, mostly. Got into a world of trouble." Pete chuckled. "Like a cheesy song. 'Got yourself into a world of trouble.'" He twisted the top off the second bottle of water, adding in an undertone, "No use tryin' to get away from myself. But I had to try."

"Oh, Pete, you're so . . . !"

"Yeah, whatever. The shit has hit the fan." He wondered why he was allowing this turn to the conversation. As far as he was concerned, his life was gone, another world. Bore no relation to his current world, doctors, nurses, hospitals, dialysis, abdominal taps, renal-friendly meals. And no substances. A few times, maybe more than a few, when he landed in a hospital, they would make him talk to psychologists, social workers, psychiatrists even. Yap yap yap. But he avoided the pitfalls, wasn't about to open up to *strangers*. Anybody. But Corina, she was in a world of trouble too. Maybe that's why he allowed her to pry.

"I know you guys pay the freight for me. Don't think I'm not grateful," he added. Wow, he was really going on tonight.

"What freight?" Corina asked.

"You know, the apartment, bills..."

"Oh, well, we couldn't not... And, we promised Mom."

"Mom," he said and sighed. Mom was the silent force. Slowly doling out cash to him. Damn! She had the money, but she acted like it was still the Great Depression or something. Like when she finally agreed to help him with the trailer—okay, when she bought the trailer—her lips were all pursed like she was worried about the next meal.

"Mom had to take you to the emergency room a bunch of times when you were little," Corina reminisced. "Remember when you fell out of that tree and broke your arm? And let's see, that baseball that hit you in the face, and, oh, other stuff. She didn't have a *car* yet when you were little. Did you know that, Pete? Dad used it for work."

"So how'd she get me to the hospital? Hitchhike?" He chuckled at the thought of prim and proper Julia Talley standing roadside with her thumb out.

"She borrowed a neighbor's, I think. A cab would have been expensive. We were almost poor then, I think."

"We were?" That was news to Pete.

"Yeah. Dad didn't hit it big until we were pretty much out of the house. That time she tried to get us to drink powdered milk instead of the real thing to save money? We just refused, remember?" Corina laughed merrily. First time Pete had heard her do that in a while.

"Yeah! I remember spitting it out 'cause it tasted like shit."

Corina looked around her and her face fell. "But this isn't my room."

Click. She was back in the new brain, synapses misfiring.

"It is your room. In a hotel. In Rincón Bay. For the family reunion." *Just the four of us left,* he added silently, thinking of all the large family reunions at Thanksgiving and Christmas in his childhood, his youth. How he would run around the backyard of whatever house they were at with the cousins he saw maybe twice a year. Usually get into what Mom called "mischief." When he was, what, thirteen, he scandalized the cousins when he pulled out a joint in the treehouse, he remembered, on a freezing December afternoon, snow thick on the ground, while the grown-ups, most of them, were getting sloshed on cocktails as they waited for the turkey to be done.

"Hey, it's late, Corina Corina," he said. He yawned. "We should get some shut-eye."

She instantly jumped into bed, became entangled in the sheets.

"Here, let me help you with that." For perhaps the first time in his life, Pete helped tuck someone in. He almost leaned over and gave her a kiss on the cheek.

"Goodnight, Corina. Sleep tight."

"Goodnight."

Back in his room, Pete took a couple of oxies.

CHAPTER 23

Toby cursed at the pain that shot through his toe when he kicked his chair in frustration. "*Fuck*. What? No, I'm not swearing at you, Becca. I just slammed my toe. Yes, it hurts but never mind that. The car . . . I can't believe it. You forgot to fill the tank? That's so not like you, Becca. Well, you're safe, that's the main thing. Um, but what about the car?"

It was the morning after the Talleys had reached Rincón Bay. Becca was surprised by the all-around recycling efficiency in Mexico. By the time the AAA tow truck got to the spot where the Mini Cooper sat, it was picked clean, as if by gigantic vultures. Ravaged.

And it had already been a crap day for Toby. He'd had two more rejections from producers. Face it, he'd thought, in the "industry," as the film business liked to call itself, he was dead meat. His toe continued to throb.

"Toby?"

"Yes?"

"Are you listening to me?"

"I am, but my toe is *throbbing.*" And nobody wants to buy my insightful ideas.

"So, tomorrow, then?"

"Tomorrow what?

"You'll come down here. You *haven't* been listening. I repeat. There were five of us in the car and all the luggage. It's impossible for Corina and Pete to be crammed in like that. We can't possibly come back in one car."

"Well, I don't have a car, remember? *We* don't have a car."

"You can rent one through All Farm. Pretty reasonable, I asked them, while our claim goes through. Or, why don't you ask Bernard to come? He can drive. That solves everything."

A gust of exasperation. "I do have work to do."

"It's the beach! You could use a break. And Toby . . ." Her voice broke and she became the hurt girl he used to know so well. "I need you."

Corina, Kathy thought, looked like a wraith. *Sunset Boulevard* in a gauzy shawl, large straw hat and big sunglasses, with a curious blend of jerky and graceful gestures. Kathy had to keep stopping for Corina and Imalia to catch up as they walked to an outdoor café nearby. It had already taken half the morning just to get her out of the posada. By the time she finally got Corina to consent to wearing a pair of leggings and sandals, Kathy was at the point of wanting to fling them at Corina's head. And now Corina, in her element, had to stop and look and listen to every single last seabird that alighted nearby.

"A blue-footed . . . bootie? No, booby," she announced proudly, pointing at the big bird. "And there's a tern. Over there, to the *right.*"

Kathy dutifully looked and told herself to be happy that Corina was happy. Wasn't that the point of this trip?

Trailing behind Imalia, who trailed Corina, came Pete. Another wraith, though no, that couldn't be the right word for the shuffling figure in the grubby T-shirt stretched over his balloon belly. Breathing hard, as if he were about to collapse.

Thankfully, the beachside café wasn't far. Pete plopped into a chair, wiped out. They ordered coffee, fruit, and little cheese pastries.

Suddenly, Corina gave a shriek. "Oh, there's a great. No, a wonderful. No. Oh, think, what is it?"

"That huge bird? Frigate bird, I think," Kathy said.

"A *magnificent* frigate bird. I am getting a bit forgetful, aren't I?"

Pete groaned. "I don't feel so good." The perennial refrain.

"Tummy?" Kathy enquired.

"Everything." He threw a half-eaten piece of melon on the sand and closed his eyes.

Corina, followed by Imalia, went closer to the shore to study the magnificent frigate bird, and in the quiet that descended, Kathy slumped. It was a beautiful day, and here was Pete, wiped out after a mere fifteen-minute walk from the posada. Which reminded her: she had to look for new accommodations.

Sighing, she got to work on her phone. But place after place was booked up. She clicked and scrolled, not seeing the pale wispy clouds arched over the aqua blue sky, the birds that whirled and pivoted over the lapping blue-green Sea of Cortez for fish, the sailboats, the bobbing waders and swimmers and the kids busy building sandcastles among the rocks.

The waiter brought more coffee and Corina and Imalia came back. Kathy's mood dropped another notch. Imalia looked uncomfortable, Corina sat as if stunned from all the bird sightings, and Pete's mouth gaped as he lolled, eyes shut, in his chair. And Becca was trying to sort out the car disaster back in the posada. Great start.

Kathy said at last, "Well, shit, everything's booked up, guys. I mean, there's a single at one place, a double at another. But we don't want to split up."

"No, we can't split up," Corina agreed, eyes round with fear.

"We'll just stay at the Carlota—it's only two more nights, and it's not really that bad, is it?"

Pete jerked awake. "What? What's bad?"

"The Posada Carlota. We have to stay there."

"Oh. That *is* bad." He wrinkled his nose.

Stop complaining, you freeloader, waster, wastrel, fuckup.

Kathy was surprised, not by her anger but by its strength. The one time in her life she'd gotten really shit-faced (not far from here; her heart raced at the thought), she'd paid a heavy price. But Pete? He'd wiggled out of consequences for decades. She'd once heard a podcast, so bizarre she remembered it clearly, how scientists had literally run a car over a bunch of insects called diabolical ironclad beetles. Diabolically ironclad: the beetles *survived* because of their mysteriously, intricately designed, force-resistant structures. Pete had been a diabolical ironclad beetle for years and years. For all the trouble he got into, nothing would pierce his denial or his trajectory. And everybody else picked up the pieces for him. How many times had her parents (Mom, really), and now she and Corina and Becca, fixed his life for him? After Julia died of a stroke, they had discussed—argued over—letting him fend for himself. But almost immediately, he'd been hit with the double whammy of a cirrhosis diagnosis and failing kidneys. They couldn't. They just couldn't abandon him.

Now, Pete turned to her. "Just teasing about the hotel. I've stayed in worse." He grinned in his slightly ghoulish way.

Kathy suddenly remembered, with a flush of shame, the same grin: when he was a little boy, always running, jumping, flying down the street on his bicycle, playing ball. Adorned with Band-Aids and casts. Crazy little brother surrounded by sisters, Dad's attention his due. And, oh so long ago, he had been a reasonably good student, enthusiastic about history. Even now, his vocabulary was surprising. How many old junkies use, and use correctly, words like "cohesive," "nonsensical," "superfluous"? Pete did. Pete!

She thought, *How did this happen? The deadness in Dad's eyes the night the sheriff's deputy came to arrest you—you were sixteen! Dad, who checked out after that, with Mom left to cope. Oh, Pete, I'm so sorry. Are you sorry? Can't you ever say you're sorry?*

Pete, as if reading her mind, said, "Sorry if I upset you, Kath. I know you're trying your best."

CHAPTER 24

Bernard pushed away from his desk, looking out the window at the narrow street of the condo complex, the blue-gray mountains with their brown and tan feet in the distance. What was it that Tamara said to him once, back in her retro-hippie phase? "I've gotta find my bliss, Dad."

When Bernard had been accepted to NYU on a full scholarship, he suggested that his dad could move out of the old neighborhood with him. Senior, who rarely showed anger, blew up at this idea. Leave his home? He had his corner stores for groceries and gossip, he had the weekly poker game with his cronies, he watched his ball games and listened to his music. So Bernard trekked back and forth between the East Village and West Orange, bringing stuff for Senior he knew was in short supply—produce, pies. Later, Kathy came along.

After they moved to Tucson, the old man did get on a plane and come for a visit. Once. He seemed to enjoy himself, but it was just the once. And they couldn't afford to go back East much, especially after the kids came along. Father and son had their weekly Sunday phone calls where they talked mostly about music. Bernard remembered one time when they had an impassioned discussion about Charlie Parker. Almost an argument. "I know you love Charlie Parker," Senior declaimed at the end, "and for sheer imaginative genius, you can't touch Bird. No. But for pure mahogany soul? Can't do better than the Hawk or Lester Young. Ben Webster too." He paused. "And that's just the saxophone. Son, those are the *giants* Bird learned from." Bernard, who loved those cats too, protested that Bird had found a new galaxy; that was all there was to it. They enjoyed these arguments, the way most guys liked to talk shit about ballplayers.

Bernard missed the long-ago times when Senior, lying back in his recliner, would call out the records, tunes, players he wanted to hear on the box. He had an old but decent sound system for his large collection of 45s and LPs. Once, back when Bernard was a raw fifteen or sixteen, he'd had the temerity to suggest his dad could make a killing if he sold those originals: Jimmie Lunceford, Count Basie, Duke Ellington, the Twelve Clouds of Joy. Senior blew his stack.

When Senior died on a day in May, Bernard didn't hear about it for two days. It was the postman, who was concerned when the mail stayed stacked up outside the door, who called the cops to check on the old man. Senior had died of a heart attack, sitting in his chair with a Best of Basie compilation still making ghost tracks on the turntable. That was thirteen years ago, and Bernard still thought of him every day. He'd gone back to Jersey alone to bury him—there was a fair crowd of the old neighborhood at the service. Not Lulu. Of course not. He'd called her and she'd said, "Oh. Well, he had a good run, though, didn't he?" He cleared out the four rooms, called

1-800-GOT-JUNK?, and shipped the records to Tucson, where those 45s and LPs had taken up a chunk of space in the living room ever since. Though Bernard seldom listened to them.

"Listen to the dynamics on this one," Senior would say from as early on as Bernard could remember. Senior was a man who valued precision for its own sake but also as the gateway to expression. "Hear how he floats right above the notes?" he'd demand, looking over his glasses at the boy as Lester Young soloed on "Lester Leaps In." "See, these guys know how to hammer you with a feather. Listen to my man Jo Jones on the drums here."

Young Bernard would pretend to understand, try not to squirm. Some years later, when his father caught him listening to a Jimi Hendrix record, he clutched his ears and removed the record, putting on something by Charlie Christian. "Now *this* is guitar playing." He also put on symphonies, Mendelssohn, Beethoven or Mozart, and he especially loved Debussy. It was all that the very young Bernard could do not to fall asleep when he played the classical stuff. One of his most vivid memories was coming to in a chair as his father was laughing at him during one of those symphonies. "Boy, you aren't ready for the masters yet, but we'll get you there." And then he sent him out to play.

Bernard sat down again and looked over what he had just written in the latest draft of the windup. "In these two prodigies, the enigma of the genius from two distinctive heritages finds common ground. Charles Parker and Wolfgang Mozart soar *beyond the constraints and values of their respective backgrounds and training into virgin territory.* Two rara avises in the ethereal language of music."

He looked out the window again. A young kid whizzed by on a bike, no hands, with a crazy happy expression.

Bernard wondered: Would he ever find his bliss?

Kathy, Corina, Imalia, and Pete waited for Becca at the beachside café, but she didn't come. Pete turned his chair around toward the beach, dozing slack-jawed, baseball cap pulled down. Corina stared at the wheeling seabirds, Imalia sat blankly beside her, and Kathy read from the book she had brought along about Frida Kahlo; it had been a birthday present from Bernard.

In her small, square room at the posada, Becca paced in ever-tightening circles as she tried to get answers from All Farm's customer-service people. "I want to talk to your supervisor" got her nowhere either; insurance didn't cover the car in Mexico. A dead loss, then. She threw the phone on the bed. This trip was supposed to be a vacation. She'd wait until she was back in the good old USA to beard the bureaucratic lion again.

But losing the Mini Cooper was more than money, though that was a big-enough hit. It was almost like losing a family member. It had taken the three of them around the country, Glacier National Park, Charleston, New Orleans, Nashville, New York. They'd maintained it, kept it clean, fed it with gas. She could—almost—cry when she thought about how, because of her oversight, it had been ravaged, how its parts would soon be sold off like illegal kidneys (if they hadn't been already). Toby was going to shit bricks when she told him they had to buy a new car.

She dropped into a chair next to Kathy when she made it to the café.

"What on earth?" Kathy asked, tapping her watch meaningfully.

"I don't want to talk about it; it'll ruin the rest of the weekend. I'll have an iced coffee, please," she told the waiter who'd appeared. She turned to Kathy. "Oh, and Toby and *Bernard* are coming down later."

"What? Why?"

Becca swept a hand over the nearly comatose-looking group. "For one thing, can you imagine the drive home with the five of us in one car?"

Kathy paused. "Okay, point taken."

"Is Tom coming?"

"No, Corina. He lives in California now."

Corina pointed at the sea. "I think I saw a *shark*. We can't go in the water."

Pete roused himself. "Did you say 'shark'?" he mumbled.

"There aren't sharks here, I read up on it," Kathy said.

"Where's Imalia?" Corina wondered.

As their late postbreakfast blurred into prelunchtime, Kathy had told Imalia to take the rest of the day off. Corina, of course, had already forgotten.

"She needed some time to herself," Kathy said. "Probably shopping."

"Or downing margaritas in a cantina," Pete suggested with a leer, then turned his chair away from them again, facing the water.

"Well, who's going to help me? I don't want strangers in my house."

"It's fine, Corina," Pete snapped. "*We* are here."

Corina tapped him on the shoulder. "It's rude to talk with your back to us. Turn around."

He muttered something, groaned, and slowly moved his chair back to face his sisters.

"So, remember the time you tried to drown me at that amusement park?" she went on. "The one with a flower name."

"Peony Park. Drown you? I didn't do that."

"Yes. You waited till I came down the water slide, and then you dunked me over and over. I was *so scared*. The lifeguard yelled at you."

"Don't remember that."

"You remember, don't you, Kathy?"

"Not really," Kathy said disloyally. She did remember. Corina was choking and crying. Julia made them go home early.

"And on Halloween you stole my trick-or-treat candy."

Don't scream, Kathy told herself. "Speaking of candy, anybody ready for lunch? Sandwiches? Tacos?"

"Yeah, then I need a nap," Pete said.

While they waited for their order, Kathy took Corina aside. "Corina. This may be the last time we'll all be together as a family. Pete..."

Corina regarded her with her blank doe eyes.

"You remember, cirrhosis, dialysis?"

"He looks terrible," Corina sniffled.

"Please? Can we just talk about the good stuff?"

"What good stuff?"

Damn, she had a point. "Well, we did have fun, sometimes... Like, when we used to play cards on the porch? And Monopoly?"

"He even cheated at Candy Land," Corina said.

Point number two. "But let's not go there. Let's try and enjoy this beautiful day."

Fortunately their food arrived then. Pete had snuck in an order of fries, definitely not a part of his renal-friendly diet. He shot Kathy a look as he ate a handful, daring her to say something.

Pick your battles, Kathy told herself. Ignoring the fries, she shifted her chair to look at the ocean as she ate her ham and cheese sandwich. The sunbathers, slick with lotion, slack against the sun, the children in their private paradise of sand. *The sand... pounding down the sand in a new ruined tunic, running in fear for her life.* Kathy gasped. *And fear of what she had left behind...*

"You all right?" Pete asked. "You look sorta out of it."

"It's nothing, just a slight headache."

"I think we should go to a casino tonight." Pete let out a tepid version of a belly laugh. "Or a cantina."

"You're joking."

"No."

"Oh, don't be ridiculous, Pete," Becca said sharply.

"What? We're here to have fun. And speaking of casinos, know what I've been thinking about, since we're all here together at a table? Let's play cards. Blackjack! Do you 'member when Mom taught us one summer at that lake? Man, what a shark she was, speaking of *sharks*, Corina. Just had to win. Out for blood, Julia was." He laughed.

"You cheated and we all knew it, but Mom wouldn't let us say anything," Corina said.

"The perfect family," Becca added.

"Not true," Pete said. "Didn't cheat. Not much."

"You always cheated. Even at Candy Land."

God give me strength. "Remember Mom's fried chicken?" Kathy said with what she hoped was a valiant attempt at brightness, Julia-style. "I've never been able to get it that crispy." *Was she getting a headache?*

"And her pies," Pete added. "Mmm."

"Those light flaky crusts," Kathy agreed. "Another thing I could never learn."

"Lemon meringue," Corina said dreamily.

"Blueberry," Becca added.

"Pecan." Kathy smiled.

"Yeah, she could bake some pies," Pete said.

Becca reached into her bag and held up a deck of cards. "Ha ha. So, you guys ready? Corina, you and I can wipe those two out easily."

"Not on your life," Pete said.

"Gin rummy," Becca said.

"Rummy it is. Pete, cut the cards."

CHAPTER 25

As Imalia walked through the dusty streets of the town behind the tourist layer, she waited for a kick of homesickness that didn't come. Yes, she was reminded of her life in Hermosillo as a girl, but she was no longer a *mexicana*. She was a *pocha*, an in-between, neither Mexican nor American; something else.

Back to business, she told herself. She planned to buy a bunch of gifts, for her sister Luchita and her nephews, Eddie, twelve, and Raimundo, nine; something of course for Nora; and maybe for herself. She stopped at a tienda for a Coke and sat at a metal table outside.

This is your patria, she told herself suddenly, *these smells, this air, this dust. Even if it doesn't feel that way anymore.* She wondered if Luchita would feel like this if she finally made the trip back to Mexico. Neither of them had wanted to return, even when they'd gotten word that their father was seriously ill after being kicked by a horse. *When the* viejo *kicks, if he ever does, we can have* una misa conmemorativa *here in Tucson*, Luchita had told her then.

All these feelings—about the señora and her brother—*dios mío*—and being here again, in the same earth where her father hung on, the old *sinvergüenza*, the shameless rogue.

The Coke perked her up. She would shop now, look for a necklace or earrings for Luchita and Nora, T-shirts for the boys. She'd go back to the posada and take a shower and then she'd see. She didn't care for the sea; in fact it put her off. She imagined sharks waiting to grab her if she even stuck her toes in the water. A wave sneaking up and taking her down to a watery grave.

No, she would rest. No one could imagine how wearing it was to care for Señora Corina, day after day. Once she had screamed and picked up a knife. Thank God, she had then thrown it on the floor. But when she ran away, into the traffic, that was the worst time. So far.

"*Ya*," Imalia declared to herself.

"*Ya*," that versatile, primal, two-letter word that could mean so many things—surprise, frustration, resignation, agreement, disbelief. In this case, enough already. Imalia asked the shopkeeper where the best jewelry shop was.

"Down the street, then take a right and you'll find it in the middle of the block. Real gold," the doughy woman behind the counter told her.

Imalia noticed the woman's gold teeth, three of them.

"All right!" Bernard took one hand from the wheel and high-fived Toby. "Welcome to the department. The treadmill."

"Thanks." Toby paused. "Wasn't for you, Matterson wouldn't have given me the new teaching job. I owe you one."

"I doubt that. Old Leo and I have diametrically opposed views."

"Nah, he respects you. Me, he thinks I'm fluff."

"He suspects anybody who goes much beyond the Fisk Jubilee Singers. Nah, it wasn't me, Tob, he's in the shit because enrollment's down."

"Ya think? When they find out the *Ring* cycle ain't *Lord of the Rings*?"

"And no offense, he's hoping your hippie stuff will bring them back." He shot Toby a grin.

"Five classes, though!" Toby said. "Well, the bread's the thing. And I won't have to work at the hardware store after the summer's over."

"Leo will ease up. What are you doing besides folk rock?"

"Well, two sets of that."

"A breeze for my man."

"And Folk Rock in Film."

"Ditto. The fifth?"

"Leo hasn't said yet." Toby paused. "The thing is, when will I have time for my own work?"

"You wanted full-time."

"I wanted *free* time. To do my own stuff."

"Well, just sayin'. No more True Value after the summer. And Becca must be dancing."

"Haven't told her yet. Once we get there. Anyway, she's way up in her own stuff right now. Well, you know."

"I do." Bernard barked a laugh.

The road was supremely monotonous, lapped by a sea of scrub desert that had long lost its allure for them. Even the lordly fat saguaros. The approaching exit advertised a Burger King.

"Pit stop?" Toby suggested.

"Sure. Fine dining too," Bernard said with a wink.

They settled into a booth in the vacant fast-food restaurant after ordering. When their order was up, they looked dispiritedly at their burgers and fries.

"Only game in town," Bernard remarked, biting into his burger.

Toby was once again fixated on the loss of the Mini Cooper. "I can't understand how Becca messed up on the gas. She's always super organized."

"Well, these aren't normal times for you guys."

Understatement, Toby thought grimly. "Your kids never got into much trouble."

"Oh, man, they had their moments. Weed, of course. Theo still smokes, I'm sure. And the Mary Jane today makes the shit we smoked seem like catnip—or so I've heard. And then, he's a little wild, well, you know about that. Tamara? She still keeps me on my toes. Last week, she told me I'm a cop-out because I don't go to those Black Lives Matter rallies. I said, 'I have been there and done that, it's your turn now.'"

But, my son's an addict, Toby thought. Wet trickled down his face. He slapped it away. "So worried about Cam." He threw down what was left of his burger. "Don't sleep. And Becca and I . . . well."

Bernard munched a fry thoughtfully. "Understandable. But you know you did the hard right thing. Got him the help he needed." He crunched another fry.

"It's put a huge strain on us. Becca and me."

One of those pauses that books call "pregnant."

"Things aren't so great with me and Kathy either," Bernard said in a casual tone that didn't fool Toby for a second. "And I didn't want her to do this trip—haul the sibs down here. She has . . . history with the place. Bad stuff."

"Kathy?" Toby cocked his head.

"Listen, don't tell her I said this. Becca either. Not that I know much. Kathy has *never* talked about it much. What I know is when she was nineteen, I think, she came down here for a spring break thing, got loaded at a beach party, and then something happened that really freaked her out."

Toby said, suddenly remembering the conversation, "Becca did mention something about Kathy having had a bad experience in college."

"And she would never come back. Always refused. I mean, unless you drive to California, where else you gonna go? The kids were so pissed, because all their friends' families went. So," Bernard sighed, "I ended up taking them. Kathy stayed in the blast furnace. And then for some reason she decides the Talley family is going to have one last shindig here?"

Toby took a swallow of Sprite. "Definitely weird." He suddenly felt very, very tired. "Hey, we've got a couple of hours left to drive: we can talk about women . . . or we can listen to music. Preference?"

"Listen to music," they said together.

After a few hands of rummy—Corina dropped out within a few minutes but seemed to enjoy watching Pete trounce their sisters—they went down to the beach. But their stay there was brief—too brief for Kathy and Becca. Pete was clearly in discomfort and Corina got weepy, so they soon trudged back to their rooms at the Carlota.

There, after a few minutes with Elizabeth Bishop's *The Complete Poems: 1927–1979*, Becca shut the book. She couldn't concentrate but she couldn't fall asleep either. She lay on her side on the sloping mattress, hands to her cheek, in what Toby called her "praying mantis" position, and let her mind wander. *Her* poetry collection would be a very short volume unless she got off the stick. She was used to what Matt Dotson, her favorite prof in college, who taught a class called Great American Poets You've Never Heard Of—so long ago now—had called the fallows, those times when a writer feels used up, burned-out, finished. This unproductive period in her writing felt unique, as if she were in a speeding car heading for a cliff. Oh Cam, oh Cam.

But at least she had the title for the book. *Tiny Vices.*

Yes. She remembered an Al-Anon meeting where she'd shared for the first time about her anger, fear, and even disgust about her father's drinking/extreme passivity and her brother's drug addiction/acting out and her mother's calm-on-the-surface, frantic rescuing of them, like juggling two broken bottles with dangerously jagged edges. It had felt like opening a bag full of decaying corpses—yes, that bad—to talk about. She shook as she spoke. Then after the meeting, some old guy in a polyester shirt, the kind she associated with grandfathers, approached her and said without preamble, "I used to think that if I close my eyes and stick my fingers in my ears, it ain't happening. She's not drunk, screeching at me that it's all my fault. I'm not disgusted about cleaning up the vomit, getting rid of the bottles, watching her snore like a buzzsaw every night. And I'm not cheating on her, I'm getting some release. And I'm not holding back with all my strength from slugging her. Then, I start coming to these meetings and I think, not facing up to all this shit is just a teeny tiny fault, that's all. Not like a real sin. Just a tiny vice, you know. But." He paused and smiled. "I kept coming here. Kept listening. And then? I knew I was killing us both by playing pretend. Don't play pretend, young lady." He shook her hand, which Becca thought was a little bizarre, and walked away.

Becca sat up. She knew, she knew when he said that, that she had to change. And with the third blow—Cam—she knew what to do. Face it. Don't justify, explain, coddle, defend. But there was so much pain. She slid back down on the bed. The book of dear, disordered, alcoholic, wonderful Bishop's poetry fell to the floor, unnoticed.

Screw having a rest, Becca thought. She needed to get out of this dank little room. She pulled on her damp swimsuit and cover-up, packed her book and sunscreen and cap and water bottle and phone, and went back to the nearby strip of sand, where she lathered herself with SPF 50. As a teenager, it was all about grilling and burning, slathered with oil. Now she girded herself against the sun. There was just enough of a breeze on the beach to make it tolerable.

Vendors wandered along the little beach here, hawking stuff. One was selling cigarettes. You could buy singles here. Imagine that. She got up and bought three cigarettes from a small, dark, strong-looking man. She'd quit twenty years ago but what the hell. No sooner had she gotten back to her towel and lit up than her phone buzzed. Toby.

"Hey," he said. "We'll be there tonight!"

"Oh, good. Reinforcements are welcome."

"Is it bad?"

"No worse than I imagined. Pete and Corina snipe at each other, Corina cries, Pete falls asleep constantly and cheats on his diet. But anyway, we're going to that big hotel on top of the cliff for dinner. Fancy, so bring your tux."

"Can we afford that?"

"Toby, don't worry about it. Corina's covering it per usual."

"Uh-huh. Right. Oh, I have news."

Becca's heart went into overtime. "About Cam?"

"No, something else."

"Nothing about Cam?"

"Well, he made his first fire. Without matches."

She took a deep breath, picturing her boy as a sober mountain man. Oh God, let him find himself. "Unbelievable, he's turning into a Boy Scout," she said, trying for lightheartedness.

"Don't you want to know what it is?"

"Know what?"

"My news!"

"Of course, but why don't you tell me when you get here." *Please, let it be a job, not another screwy idea about the lives of middle-management mafiosos on Long Island or a guitar player nobody's heard of.*

When Becca made it back to her room, she pulled out her notebook without thinking and wrote,

> *Golden wings flung at the white sky*
> *The sun eating itself like honey*
> *Wings, limbs, white sky,*
> *Wanting to fly,*
> *I am freckled and drooping,*

I want to fly
Water, rocks and I
meld with the sky,
the sun eats itself like honey

She closed the notebook and closed her eyes and drifted into one of those half daydream, half dreams where she and Corina and Kathy and Pete were dancing in a circle on the beach. Then she realized that Pete was not her brother, he was a stranger; no, a doppelgänger. The sun was dripping, no, she was sweating. They were singing something—she couldn't hear it. Was it a song she wrote? *It's mine!* yelled the Pete stand-in. *Mine!* Becca gasped at his anger, but she was asleep.

Later, she stirred and checked her phone. How had she slept that long? It was time to get ready for dinner.

She heaved herself up off the bed and checked herself out in the bathroom mirror. Hair? Frizzier than she liked, but this was the beach, after all. Now those circles under her eyes, were they still concealable? She showered, put on her blue-and-white-striped tunic dress, combed her hair into waves, applied makeup.

Not too bad, she thought.

Toby would be here soon. She didn't know how she felt about that. He was a good man; she was his pain in the ass. She carried the water, though.

She put on her little dangling turquoise earrings and nodded with approval at her reflection. A nice touch.

She had spent the day with her family, she had started a poem. She had finally slept. That was something.

CHAPTER 26

Imalia hadn't shown up by six, when they had planned to leave for Azul. Kathy felt a small brush of worry but decided that maybe Imalia had misunderstood and thought she was getting the night off too.

Becca and Kathy met in the hall.

Kathy frowned. "Where's Corina?"

"I thought she would be with you," Becca said. "Oh shit, is Imalia back yet?"

They went to Corina's room. She was sitting on her bed in her underwear. "I'm hot."

It was true that the air conditioning at the posada left a lot to be desired. Kathy tamped down her annoyance as she said, "Come on. Get dressed, it's time to go."

"Go where?"

"A beautiful restaurant, remember? Let's see, how about these?" She held up a pair of pale blue jeans.

"Oh no, no."

"Then these," Becca said, handing her black linen pants.

"No, I don't think so."

"Well, the only other choice is your yoga pants, which have a stain on them—see?"

"That's all I brought?" Corina looked crushed.

They got her into the black pants, a top, and sandals. Kathy brushed her hair, noting sadly that her once meticulously groomed sister really needed a shampoo. And she had lost interest in makeup.

They went to the dinky lobby, where Pete waited. At least he'd put on a clean shirt. But he'd also thrown on his old Diamondbacks baseball cap. Maybe he'd take it off at the restaurant. Whatever; Kathy was beyond caring.

"Where's Imalia?" he asked.

"She must have made other plans," Becca said.

"With Nora," Corina said. "They're lovers, you know."

Pete snorted. "You already blew their cover."

"Let's move on," Becca said.

"I think it's wonderful for them, " Corina said stoutly.

Pete rolled his eyes.

"What are we waiting for? Let's go," Becca said.

"Where are we going?" Corina asked anxiously.

"We're having dinner at Azul, on top of the cliffs."

"Oh! I'd better change then. This outfit won't do." Corina turned and started walking back to her room.

Kathy went after her. "It's the beach. It's casual. You look perfect." She wrapped an arm around her and steered her back toward the lobby. "Come on."

As they drove next to the bay, the Pedroso de Oro Hotel glowed at the far end like a mirage. Steep cliffs plunged to the sea on three sides of the ornate edifice, in what could be called the *cartelism* or *cartelismo* style: basically, launder as many of the ill-gotten gains as possible in various combinations of over-the-top decor.

Kathy's stomach clenched as she drove along the cliffs. *It must have been around here,* she thought. But in place of the scrub desert of all those years ago, there were houses, condos, huts. Only a few expanses of desert remained. But it was along this way, she knew. There was nowhere else it could have happened.

She turned to look at the sea, glinting and darkening as the sun set. People were still lazing on the beach, swimming, children were running around, a few vendors still wandered around, looking for last pickings. Feeling a tug of dread at this peaceful, ordinary scene, she turned to look again at the sparse bits of desert that remained. Something flashed—the sun hitting a beer can, that's all, she told herself. She heard screams and realized she'd swerved off the road. She stopped the car.

"What the hell? What's the matter with you? Are you sick? You look like you're going to be sick."

"I don't know. Yes."

Kathy leaned out of her door. Had dry heaves.

"Deep breaths!" Becca told her.

After a few moments, Kathy said, "Okay. I'm good now."

"Well, get in the passenger seat. I'm driving," Becca told her. "We'll go back to the posada. Maybe you have food poisoning."

"No, no, I just got lightheaded, maybe a little dehydrated. Too much sun, not enough water. I'll be fine, Becca. Just drive. This is our big night out as a family."

"Okay then," Becca said dubiously, adding below her breath, "and, oh, what a family it is."

Kathy turned around to the back. "I'm fine. Just, you know, one of those weird moments, too much sun. I'm good now."

"You almost made us crash!" Pete said loudly.

Becca winced. "Pete, Pete, cool it."

They continued the rest of the way in silence. Becca parked on the drive below the hotel. They had to walk up a steep flight of stairs, stopping every few steps to wait for Pete.

"This place is super fancy," he wheezed when they got to the top, sweeping an arm around the marbled, intricately tiled lobby. "Cartel chic!" He snickered.

"Ooh, is this where we're going to stay?" Corina asked. And for a moment, she looked uncannily like her old glamorous self.

"We're going to the restaurant," Becca reminded her.

They went up and up in a glittering elevator, then stepped out onto a massive terrace overlooking the bay.

Azul was quite full, but the tables were set wide apart. A sleek young Mexican woman led them to theirs, which Kathy thought looked like a great, carved sheet of ice topped with gold placemats and a steep pottery bowl filled with masses of birds-of-paradise.

"Sure beats Burger King," Pete said.

Corina stared at him. "Take that cap off. It's dreadful!"

"No."

"It's so tacky. I'm ashamed to be sitting with you."

Bernard and Toby appeared.

"Oh wow, you made it!" Becca jumped up. "We weren't sure you would."

"No traffic," Bernard said.

"Floored it all the way," Toby added.

"Let's get you chairs and some more of these fancy place settings," Kathy said. "Where's the waiter?"

"*Waitperson*," Pete said and snickered.

Bernard stood, hands in his pockets, looking around with his eyebrows raised.

"Fancy," he said.

"Hey." Kathy got up and gave him a hug. He returned it in a cursory way.

"All good?" he asked.

"Um... I'll tell you later," she said, sotto voce.

Two chairs were soon delivered, followed by two large pottery bowls with guacamole and chips.

After having his first bite, Pete said, "Why do they bother with all this African and Asian stuff on the menu? Mexican is the bomb."

Dipping and crunching, the extended Talley clan seemed then like just another big family on vacation. But even as she smiled and made small talk, Kathy felt she was on the edge of something, as if the desert below was waiting for her. Deep breaths, as Becca had reminded her.

They all ordered fish as their entrées, except Pete, who wanted an ill-advised cheeseburger, and Toby, who decided to have the *birria de chivo al estilo marrueca*—Moroccan- style goat stew.

A breeze flowed and a trio in the corner strummed guitars and their drinks arrived.

So far, so good, Kathy thought.

Becca leaned over to her. "Everybody's behaving themselves," she said, low. "I guess we did it."

Before Kathy could reply, Corina asked, "Why did we order? We should wait for Tom!"

"Tom again? You got a divorce, don't you remember?" Pete shook his head. "Memory like a sieve."

Kathy kicked Pete under the table. "What?" he said loudly.

"We got divorced, that's right. Because he couldn't keep his dick in his pants!"

"Corina!" Becca and Kathy exclaimed together.

"Well, it's true. And you know what he told me? Back when he was in Catholic school, the nuns terrified him so much about masturbating that he said he couldn't touch himself after that. They didn't say anything about not *having sex* though. Probably couldn't imagine that. So, Tom said he decided it was okay for him to sleep around, since he was away from me so much. Just part of doing business!"

Kathy's gaze landed on Bernard just as he and Toby exchanged *Get me out of here* looks. She couldn't really blame them.

"Well, I liked Tom," Pete said.

"Pete, leave it, she's upset," Bernard muttered.

"Why? I admit he had his faults, but he was a generous guy. Bought me those Bose speakers."

Corina stared at him. "You've always liked tormenting me." She began to cry.

Pete glared back. "Just telling it like it is."

Toby and Bernard downed their beers at almost exactly the same moment, while Becca and Kathy tried to soothe Corina.

As in most overpriced restaurants, the food, artistically arranged and ungenerously sized, took a long time to arrive.

But it was delicious. Everyone except Corina turned to their meals enthusiastically.

"Let's order dessert and coffee!" Kathy said in a strangely chirpy voice once they'd finished.

"Yeah! I'm having flan. Flan's the only dessert they have in Mexico," Pete said.

"That is so not true and you're diabetic, so forget about dessert," Becca responded sharply.

Kathy heard Bernard groan, and she shot him a half-angry, half-beseeching look.

Corina had calmed down again, was placidly eating tiny bites of cake. Pete, toying with the slices of mango that were his dessert, smiled secretively; he'd had ice cream that afternoon, a double dip, chocolate and strawberry. Still, he couldn't help but feel deprived as he watched the others at the table scarf down the flan or chocolate cake that was the house specialty.

When he closed his eyes, his irritation faded as he focused on listening to the waves breaking against the rocks below, louder than the ambient noises of the busy restaurant. He felt himself drifting and the waves became the waves of sound from a crowd at a stadium where he was high up in the cheap seats. With Allen, Billy, Crazy Joe, and Billy's lame cousin whose name nobody ever remembered. They were sixteen or seventeen.

"Ah man, this is gonna be fuckin' great."

"Best ever. Eddie fuckin' Halen."

Tiny figures appeared far below on the stage and then an awesome smash of chords ... WTF? Crazy Joe was *puking*.

"Don't get any of that on me, asshole! The concert's *started*, man, cool it."

CJ's eyes were rolling around and he was out as the music began. (They poked and prodded him to make sure he was still among the living.) Van Halen was on fire! Crashing waves . . . Before he was sent to juvie. Before he got turned on to Beefheart and Zappa and . . .

Someone was poking him. "What, what?" He opened his eyes, thought, *Oh, the girls.* "Musta have drifted off for a sec."

"Your face was almost in your *plate*." Corina frowned. "Are you all right?"

"Ready to go now," he mumbled.

"We're waiting on Kathy and Becca," Bernard said.

"Where are they?" Corina pouted. "They didn't ask me to go with them."

"They went to the ladies'," Toby said.

Bernard looked at his watch. "Fifteen minutes ago."

Becca and Kathy were walking down the long hallway from the restroom when Becca stopped at a little balcony over which a three-quarters-full moon was shining, the sea below silver and gold. "What a great view. Let's sit here a moment."

She sat on a bench. Kathy leaned over the railing, staring at the large rock formation below. It was the only large natural structure along that long sweep of sand. Her heart began to race.

Becca came to the railing. "Wow, what a moon!"

Kathy tried to respond but she couldn't speak. She was remembering. How she and J had danced around that rock tower. They were singing—what? Oh, yes: Joni Mitchell's "The

Circle Game"—and suddenly, it was as if someone had taken a giant bottle of Windex and wiped the encrustations off her memory.

It was thirty years ago, but she could see that curvy young woman in the embroidered Mexican tunic she'd thrown over her bikini, and J, the round-faced girl with green-tipped hair. And she could—almost—feel the rocks on the spire, alternately deeply pitted and smoothly worn as she ran her hands over the surface—high and feeling free—before . . . Before she was slammed to the ground. As a boy, or a man, lunged at her again. She almost froze but she got an arm free of his grasp and—her memory clouded over again but she willed it back—then she yanked the hard metal key of her hostel room that she was wearing around her neck on a string and the string broke and she stabbed the key at his face. There was a scream, he stumbled away, and she saw blood gushing down his face. From his eye. As she fell flat on her back in the sand.

She heard another high-pitched, shrill scream. J.

And then Kathy was up and running. She stumbled, regained her footing. She must get away. Back to the crowd, the bonfire. Safety.

But she couldn't see what happened next. She must have sought help. She wouldn't have abandoned J, would she? But she just couldn't remember anything after that. Did she pass out?

Then she woke up in her room at the hostel and it was light out. She was still in the Mexican tunic. It was ripped, and stained. With blood? She threw up, then showered, threw her stuff together. Left the tunic in a trash can. She walked to the little bus depot and waited for the next bus back to Tucson.

"You okay?" Becca asked.

Kathy jumped. "No. Give me a minute." *Anne said this could happen. 'Be gentle with yourself,' she'd said.*

She wept while Becca sat quietly, letting her have her moment.

Kathy gulped the clean sea air, wiped her eyes, said she didn't want to talk about it yet. They went down the gleaming hall back to the restaurant.

Becca kept shooting looks at her, but she didn't say anything.

CHAPTER 27

Amalia decided to take a rare nap when she came back from shopping. Just a short snooze; even that felt like a luxury.

But it was dark out when she woke up. She looked at the time on her phone. Dios mío, *I missed their big dinner. It's nearly eight o'clock!* But after that brief moment of panic, she smiled. Perhaps the señora would save her the trouble of having to quit her job, as she planned to do soon enough. A new life waited for her in Tucson with Nora. She could find another job, as a housekeeper or maybe in the cantina. Yes, that would be fine.

Hungry, she went to the courtyard where they supposedly served food, but as before it was deserted. She found the night watchman in the kitchen, watching a telenovela on his phone, a bottle of beer on the table. Yes, he told her, the gringos had left two hours ago. And yes, he'd let her make a sandwich.

She ate it on the patio, then called Nora.

"I've made up my mind," she told her. "I'm going to tell them I'm leaving. In two weeks. And I'll tell Luchita I'm moving out." *I am thirty-nine and I have never had a place of my own. I have never lived with a lover.*

Nora told her she had thought it over, that yes, they should open up a place together, not to compete with Lola's, not a bar. "Norima's," she said. "A café. Coffees and juices, *licuados*, delicious Mexican pastries. Books. Like *Borderlands/La Frontera*." She'd even begun a business plan.

"Wonderful!" Imalia said. She wouldn't have to worry anymore about the señora. Or Luchita. No one but herself. And Nora. "I love it," she said. "It's perfect."

"You're perfect," Nora purred.

"Too fat."

"Love handles, *mi amor*."

"Goodnight, *querida*," Imalia said, smiling into the phone.

In the town that afternoon, Imalia had seen a bar that reminded her of Lola's. She was going to go there and celebrate, yes. Fully refreshed after the nap and the chicken-and-avocado sandwich.

She put on a fresh blouse and pants and went out into the soft night.

Azul was getting raucous, tables now full and the bar three deep, the margaritas and the mojitos and the Coronas flowing and the mariachis jamming at the far end of the balcony.

At the Talley table, still minus Kathy and Becca, there was a more subdued vibe. Bernard and Toby had polished off their cake and were sipping coffee with rum. Pete picked at his mango, and Corina stared at the spectacular spray of yellow-and-red-flowered birds-of-paradise in the vase in the middle of the table. Then she began to whimper.

"What now? Would you stop?" Pete leaned toward her. He handed her a paper napkin. "You're embarrassing everybody," he muttered.

"Tom used to give me the most beautiful bouquets on my birthday, anniversaries, any time we had a fight," she said. "I miss him. Don't you miss Charlotte?"

Pete jerked back in his chair. Charlotte? Corina remembered *Charlotte*? She barely remembered her own name now. And yes, he still thought at times about Charlotte, but he hadn't thought much about her in a while, not since he had all this medical shit to deal with.

He'd met her when he was on a job, during the brief period he was gainfully employed as an air conditioner repairman. They'd hit it off right away. Chicks didn't do it for him usually. Too demanding. But Charlotte was different. She wasn't a ballbuster and she liked to party. Okay, she had two little kids, but nothing was perfect. When he and Charlotte hung out, she would send them to the playground at her apartment complex or the trailer park or plopped them in front of the TV with snacks.

He and Charlotte got high, sure, but they did things too. Charlotte would cook, nothing fancy but still. They took Annie and Jake to the park. To McDonald's. Once, they even went to the Desert Museum. There was some kids' program that day and he'd bought them all stuff at the gift shop, Charlotte a bracelet, stuffed animals for Annie and Jake. After that weekend, Pete thought he'd ask her to move in with him full-time. Maybe get a bigger trailer down the line.

But the next weekend Charlotte didn't show up or call and he was alternately pissed off and worried that something had happened to her. So he went to her crummy apartment complex, but there was no answer when he knocked. A maintenance guy with broken English passing by was the one who told him: Charlotte was dead. The kids had been running around outside in the middle of the night and someone called the cops and they found Charlotte OD'd, the guy added, sliding his eyes away. The kids had been taken away.

"*Bullshit!*" Pete had shouted, as the guy hurried away.

"Yeah," he told Corina in a gravelly voice, "I think about her sometimes." He wiped his eyes with the back of his hands and bent his head.

Further down the table, Bernard turned to Toby. "Look at those two, blubbering. Where the hell are our wives?"

Toby shook his head, got up, went around the table, put his hand on Corina's shoulder, and nodded at Pete. "Anything I can get you guys? More cake? Pete, some fruit? Coffee?"

They both shook their heads without looking at him, and then they did look up, as Becca's soft voice asked, "What's all this?"

Kathy, sinking into her seat, said nothing, but she took Corina's hand and rubbed it.

"Why are *you* crying, Corina? You're rich. You can have anything you want," Pete said much too loudly.

"Don't, Pete!" Kathy said so harshly that nearby diners turned and looked at her.

"It's true," he said plaintively.

Toby said, "Sensory overload," and shook his head slightly at Kathy and Becca in a *What-were-you-thinking?* bobble.

Kathy took a quick breath. "Oh, I'm so over this. Tote that barge, Kathy, lift that bail!"

"Kathy." Bernard's voice was low but authoritative.

Kathy flung up her arms. "I'm leaving!" She ran clumsily out of the room.

"I'll get the check, you go after her," Toby said. "See you downstairs."

Bernard heaved a sigh, rose, and strode away.

There was silence at the table then until the check, a monstrously large sum, appeared. Becca peered at it and whispered to Toby, "Just put it on the card. I'll get it from Corina's account."

"Becca—"

"Don't start, Toby."

The hefty charge taken care of, Toby, Becca, Corina, and Pete walked through the laughing, shouting, singing, drinking restaurant down the silent hall to the silent elevators and through the quiet lobby down the long, twisting marble stairs to the road. Becca had an arm around bird-boned Corina; Toby kept an eye on tottery Pete. Bernard and Kathy were standing apart and seemed to be arguing.

"We're all feeling emotional tonight," Toby heard Becca reassure Corina as she guided her toward the car. "It's all right, we're going home now, back to the posada."

"What was that?" Bernard was barely in the door.

Kathy slumped on the bed in their room at the posada.

"You just take off? You saw how upset your sister was. And your brother. What a shock," he added grimly.

"I know, I know! But. I *remembered*, Bernard. What happened here. I finally *know*. And it was too much. I just couldn't deal with . . . them."

Bernard flopped into the chair and waited.

She looked up. Not at him. Beyond him, speaking very fast. "And the funny thing is, it feels like I've always known."

"Well, how did you . . . I mean, what made you remember?"

"That rock spire. The only one, that tall one. Becca and I, when we went to the bathroom, on the way back, we were looking over this balcony and—it was like I was *there*. Nineteen again. With this other girl. All I remember is her name started with a *J*—Joan, Jill, Jackie?"

"Yeah, you said that before, when you had a nightmare and I had to wake you up. You were screaming, 'J!'"

"Well, tonight, I could *see* us. I could see the two of us, goofing around on that rock spire. Singing, laughing, drinking warm beer. And then . . . they just came at us, these two guys . . . One of them grabbed me, and J . . . I guess the other guy had J. But my dress ripped, and I broke free and I, I grabbed my hotel key . . . this big old-fashioned key, for the hostel. It was on a string around my neck. So I wouldn't lose it. And I jabbed it at him, as hard as I could, and it went in his face. His eye. I felt it. Oh God."

Kathy sank to the floor, covering her eyes. Bernard had to strain to hear her now.

"It went in his *eye*. He was howling. I saw blood. A lot of blood. And J was screaming too . . . Then, I started to run. Down the beach. So fast. You know I'm a lousy runner. But I could have beat Usain Bolt. And then, I . . ." She sobbed softly. "Oh my God, I stabbed him in the eye and I left her there."

"Kath, Kath." Bernard came and put his arm around her. Her skin felt like it was on fire.

"I left her there, Bernard! She was yelling for help!"

"But you ran for help." Of course she did. That's who Kathy was.

"Did I? I don't know! Because there's nothing after that. Just blank. " Her voice dropped to a whisper. "Until I woke up the next day in my room at the hostel. So I was at least able to do that. Or someone helped me. *I don't know, Bernard.* Then I went to the bus stop and I left. I didn't even ask anybody if they'd heard about a girl—J—if she was okay, what happened to her. *What happened to her?*" She paced around the little room.

"You would have told someone. You know you would. You *rescue* people, Kathy, that's what you do."

She whirled around. "I left her alone with those monsters! And I wouldn't let myself think about it, about what might have happened to her. I just wanted to get away."

"You fought for your life! You did what you had to do!"

Eventually she calmed down enough to fall asleep, but Bernard couldn't. He lay awake in the dark. He wondered if *he* was a monster. Of course, he felt bad for her. What she'd gone through was horrible. But all these years of avoiding it had taken a toll on him too. On their marriage. And now, all these problems with the family. Her family. Corina, Pete, Cam. He was so tired of Talley drama.

Bernard let his mind drift where it wanted. To a life apart, a life where there was no drama but his own. Yes, he had his own demons. His chest tightened. He had loved her, he loved being a father. But now? He didn't know. He was so tired of his life.

He pictured a cabin in the mountains, the sounds of birds, wind, rain. Music whenever he wanted, as loud as he wanted, at three in the morning. Art Blakey and the Jazz Messengers. Otis Redding. Stevie Wonder. Beethoven. Or just silence, all around him. God, was he turning into his father?

Then he too was asleep.

CHAPTER 28

Becca tried to wake Toby, who lay on his back with limbs sprawled and mouth gaping, his Do Not Disturb position.

After several sharp shakes, he bolted straight up. "What? What? What?"

"Do you hear that loud noise? Like someone is crashing around."

They looked at each other.

"Pete?" Toby guessed, then groaned.

Becca threw on her robe and flew out the door, Toby behind her. They knocked at Pete's door, tried it. Locked. Nothing.

"Get a key!" she said. Toby ran to the lobby. "Pete? Pete! Answer me."

Kathy and Bernard appeared, neither looking well. Thankfully, Corina was sleeping through the commotion.

Toby came back. Keyless. No one at the desk, per usual. "We're gonna have to break the door down," he said.

"No, man, this ain't the movies," Bernard protested.

"We have to go in," Kathy snapped.

Bernard's face cleared. "There's a window. We go outside and break the glass. That I can handle."

Toby and Bernard and Kathy rushed outside and Becca continued staring at the door, half wanting to run away, to grab her car keys and . . . *Oh, that's right, I don't have a car anymore. Pete, Pete, don't be dead.* She banged on the door. She tapped on the door. She yelled through the door. She whispered. And then she heard the smash at the window and a groan.

Pete was on the floor, semiconscious and confused.

"A hospital," Kathy said. "There's gotta be one in this town."

Wordlessly, Toby and Bernard worked to get Pete on his feet. They half carried him outside to Bernard's car, then dashed back inside to throw on some pants and lock up. Becca had pulled on shorts and a T-shirt and was looking for a hospital on her phone while Kathy went to tell Corina, in case she woke up and they weren't there.

Just as Becca found an address, Kathy showed up at her door with Corina.

"She insisted on coming too," Kathy said.

Surprise, Becca thought.

Becca found an address and the sisters took off, Kathy driving, Becca feeding her directions, Corina thankfully silent, with a deer-in-the-headlights look in the back. Toby and Bernard followed them, Pete lying down on the back seat.

I should be driving, Becca thought as they sped along. *Kathy's freaked out. And she's driving too fast.*

"I was mean to Pete, and now he's going to die," Corina said tearfully.

"Oh, Corina, no! He was eating bad stuff all day and probably fucked up his blood sugar," Becca said. "Look out for Avenida de los Pescadores," she added to Kathy. "It should be coming up."

It wasn't. They stopped for Kathy to ask directions in Spanish from a vendor dozing beside his cart. He thought there might be a clinic ahead and, sure enough, soon they saw a whitewashed building with a single light on outside a darkened entrance with a sign, Unidad de Medicina Familiar 8.

They got out of the car as the guys pulled in behind them.

"This is it?" Bernard asked. "It's dinky. Is it even open?"

"It's gotta be open if it's a hospital," Kathy said. "Bang on the door."

Just then a thin man in a Mexican cowboy hat emerged, leaning on an equally thin woman in a faded flowered dress, like something out of *The Grapes of Wrath*.

They swept past the couple and took Pete inside. Kathy went over to a tired-looking woman in scrubs who was standing between the small waiting room and a hallway.

"*Mi hermano es muy enfermo, es un diabético y también tiene*—damn, what's the word for 'cirrhosis' in Spanish?—*cirhotico? Y otras cosas...*"

The woman made the quintessential Mexican gesture of acquiescence to the fates and pointed down a short hallway. Pete shuffled between Bernard and Toby to a small room. So small it was standing room only.

Kathy went back and had a brief discussion with the woman, whose nameplate said she was Dr. Maduro. Maybe the only doctor there at night. Kathy returned to the room.

"They don't take Medicaid," she told them.

"Fuck this place, then," Pete rasped, now in a wheelchair that Toby had managed to find and brought back. "Let's go back to the good old US of A."

"No, no." Kathy reassured him. "It's free! We don't have to pay anything. *Nada*."

"Nada?" Pete repeated. He began to laugh and then cough.

"I don't know," Becca hedged, "it seems pretty basic for Pete's, uh, issues."

"It's the best there is right now," Bernard inserted, "so let's get him seen to. Look at the man!" he added in an undertone.

Pete, white as a sheet, was still coughing.

Kathy ran out of the room. Shortly afterward, a male doctor who looked too young to be one came in and banished the family to the waiting room with not enough plastic chairs and an empty fish tank.

In his room, a nurse showed up to help Pete undress and get him onto the hospital bed. "What's all this?" he mumbled as she set up his intubation. She shot him a keen look as she stuck a needle in his arm. Ah . . . morphine. He closed his eyes and fell into warm liquid, and someone was splashing him. Peony Park! His favorite place as a little kid on those endless summer days. The lifeguards shouted and blew their whistles at what seemed like an enormous pool to young Pete. Then Pete thought he was ready for ice cream, or no, a root beer float. But he couldn't seem to get out of the water; in fact he realized he was going under.

After a blank eternity, he came up for air, gasping.

He opened his eyes to brown faces looking at him and remembered he was in a hospital again. Okay, he knew this drill. But wait, this was Mexico. Where was the family? Just the girls now. He missed them desperately, he realized, Corina, Kathy, Becca. He knew he had crashed again. Would they please quit jabbering at him in Spanish? I don't understand, *comprende?* Get Kathy, she speaks the lingo. I want to go home. Just patch me up so I can get in the recliner, watch a show, eat one of those renal-friendly frozen dinners. Yum yum. Rest up and then work on the new tune...

His sisters were back. "Becca, Kathy, he's smiling, I think. Pete? It's us. Your sisters." Corina's face came into focus.

"I know that," he mumbled.

"He hears us! Pete? We're here, we're not going anywhere."

"Remember Peony Park?" he asked.

"Not that again," Kathy murmured, shooting Becca a look. Becca raised her eyebrows.

"What?" Corina looked confused for a moment, but then she ventured, "The public pool when we were kids?"

"You scraped your knee on the bottom of the pool and I got you a snow cone. Corina? Man, could you holler."

"I don't remember that."

"Or maybe it was a popsicle." He let out a long sigh and closed his eyes again.

They had been waiting at the clinic for hours, which turned out to do a surprising amount of business for such a humble-seeming place. A man came in with an arm wrapped in rags, dripping blood all over the floor, another man with a little girl who was vomiting into a plastic container, a pregnant woman shrieking. Finally, finally, the same, now even-more-tired-looking doctor-administrator took them to Pete's room.

"He has many diseases, but first of all, he is diabetic," she told Kathy in Spanish.

"Oh yes, as I said, he's on dialysis."

"Well, he was going into a coma."

"Could you speak slowly, please? I speak basic Spanish but..."

"His blood sugar was out of control," the doctor said slowly. "Plus, there are complications from his liver. As soon as he's stabilized, he must go to a bigger facility."

Kathy turned to Pete, who was still pale and listless but better. "What did you eat, Pete? I know you had ice cream this afternoon, damn it. Did you eat any of that cake at the restaurant?"

Pete turned his head away. "Hey, I'm on vacation, I caved. Stupid."

"What the fuck, Pete?"

CHAPTER 29

As she had when she went to Lola's Cantina the first time and saw women laughing and hugging and kissing, Imalia almost turned around and left the bar in Rincón Bay. Once again, though, she made herself go in, walk up to the bar, order a cerveza, and look around, ignoring the trembling inside. (If her father knew, if her brother knew, if anyone knew! Flinging insults at her: *camionera, lechuga, lencha, queer.*) She thought of Nora, how that first time at Lola's, Nora had come to her, that beautiful Mayan *huipil*, those amber eyes, that big smile.

This bar was not as nice as Lola's, not as clean, but people said *hola* and soon she'd accepted a drink and ended up sitting at a table with laughing women, trading shots of tequila.

She woke up in a *choza*, a shack, could have sworn before she opened her eyes that she was back home at the ranchito. The roosters, the adobe, the smell. She regarded with wonder the cramped room and the face of the woman with the spill of raven hair beside her, asleep under a blanket, having no memory of getting here last night. But here she was.

Cautiously, she dressed and tiptoed out, looking straight ahead in the lane, her head hurting. She wanted water, but she didn't want to stop, so she plodded on until she saw a little plaza around which a couple of taxis were parked, their drivers dozing. "La Posada Carlota," she told one. Numbly, she watched the lazy streets go by.

Once at the posada, she reached in her bag to pay the driver but found nothing but a wadded Kleenex. Cleaned out. Thank God, she had not brought her credit card.

Mexico, you beautiful, ugly, merciless pit, taking, robbing, needing, bleeding, I will be done with you only when I die.

"I need to go get some money," she told the driver, who followed her, as if he were used to being ripped off, even in broad daylight.

But not only was Señora Corina not there; no one else was there either. Except the receptionist, for once. "Yes, the señores were here a little while ago. They said they needed to get some things for their brother who is in a hospital . . . Yes, they told me. Unidad de Medicina 8 . . ." Imalia turned to the glowering cabbie. "*Dios mío*. Take me there, please."

At the clinic, the man followed her inside again. "This is costing me plenty, lady," he growled.

"I know, I know. Oh!" she appealed to a tired-looking woman, "I'm trying to find some *norteamericanos*?"

"Wait here." The woman went off to fetch someone.

El prieto, the dark-skinned, handsome husband of Señora Kathy, came to the lobby.

"Oh, señor, *perdoneme*. Today all my money took, I must to pay this *taxista*. Please, will you lend me—How much, señor?" she asked, turning to her shadow.

"A hundred pesos," he said.

After some rapid-fire Spanish, the cabbie agreed to take sixty-five.

"I will pay it back, señor," Imalia said anxiously.

Señor Bernard looked confused for a moment. "Oh. Sure." He reached in his pocket, stopped, laughed sheepishly. "Sorry, I left my wallet at the hotel. I'll go get some from Kathy or somebody."

He left, returning with a fifty-peso bill and five US dollars.

The driver grabbed the money and, a satisfied expression on his face, vanished.

"So, Corina could use your help right now," Bernard told Imalia.

Imalia could hear the all-too-familiar sound of the señora's wails; she'd recognize that sound anywhere. She felt like wailing too. Her head ached and she was numb with guilt.

But it was just un pequeño vicio, *just a little sin. And I remember almost nothing about it! Doesn't that make it less bad? (The shots of tequila and whirling to the rancheras that blasted in that hot cantina, some hot kisses, body slick with sweat, winding little streets, laughter . . .)*

The Unidad de Medicina Familiar 8 was professionally vague about when Pete could be released. Tomorrow? Probably not. There was a dialysis center on the other side of town—something of a miracle for most small Mexican communities, but Rincón Bay had a sizeable expat community. If need be, Pete could be sent there and then back to No. 8 until he was deemed fit to travel. Meanwhile, since none of the family had slept or eaten since Azul, they decided to go to the café they liked near the posada and then crash for a while.

Except for Bernard. "Nah," he said, "I'll just pick up a breakfast burrito or something, then take a snooze." He waved a hand and left.

"What's up with him?" Becca murmured. "He seems awfully... strange."

Kathy sighed. "Long story."

"Well, the rest of us can go then," Becca said quickly, clearly not interested in any more drama for now.

They piled into the car. At the café, they ate quickly. Sleep, on those lumpy mattresses, that's what they craved.

Kathy expected to find Bernard passed out at the posada, but he wasn't there. Running on the beach, she was sure. *Don't you get sunstroke*, she thought drowsily before sinking into oblivion.

A knock at the door an unmeasurable amount of time later woke her up. A nervous Imalia. That could mean only one thing.

"*Señora Corina está muy agitada*," she confirmed.

Kathy sighed and went to Corina's room.

Corina was still draped in her old kimono. She flew at Kathy, imploring, "Can we take Pete and get out of here?"

"We need to wait for them to stabilize him first."

"I want to see him!"

Kathy looked at her watch. She had slept two hours. She sighed. "All right. Put some clothes on, Corina. These shorts. Imalia, is there a clean T-shirt? Yes? And sandals."

"And water bottles," Corina said.

"They're in the cooler. I put it in my room," Kathy said. "We'll get some on our way out."

"I need one now."

"Well, I need a big fat latte. Actually, I need a big fat glass of wine! I need a private plane to get me out of here! I need—"

Corina gasped. "You're yelling at me!"

Kathy bent her head. *Breathe, breathe.* "We'll go to that café," she said quietly.

"But I want to see Pete!"

Kathy raised her voice again, though not as much. "For the love of God, Corina, half an hour won't make a difference. He's probably sleeping anyway."

Corina's face fell. "You keep yelling at me. I can't help it, you know. I wish I could."

"Oh God, honey, I'm sorry. I just—I have—a lot on my mind."

"Mind? Oh yes, that," Corina said. Sitting in the wicker chair with the faded cushions in the little box of a room, that vague look came into her eyes. "I wish I had a new mind and a new home. But not here. No."

"You have a lovely home back in Tucson."

The easy tears gushed. "I do, don't I?"

Kathy hugged her tight. *You can do this. You can be there for them. And then when you get home, you can fall apart.* "Corie, Corie." The childhood nickname she hadn't used in decades. "Come on now. It's a beautiful day. We'll have coffee or water or iced tea or whatever you want, then we'll see Pete."

She helped Corina into the T-shirt she was struggling with. Imalia, hovering, brought her sandals and bent to strap them on.

Standing beside her spectral sister, Kathy felt her heart tighten at the childlike way Corina was submitting to being dressed. Soon she would not be able to feed herself, wash herself. Oh God.

"Where's Becca?" Corina wondered.

"Sleeping or whatever in her room. I'll go get her." But there was no answer at Becca's door. Probably taking a walk, Kathy thought.

Kathy, Corina, and Imalia walked to the café again, the sea shallow and lazily lapping nearby, glittering, primeval.

But Becca was already at the café, at "their" table, glumly drinking her own latte. Kathy raised an eyebrow at her. Becca shook her head.

Kathy ordered a large bottle of water, coffee. "Shall we have some pastries too?" she asked.

"But don't order salad," Corina warned Kathy. "You can get *turista*."

"We're not having salad," Kathy said, suppressing yet another sigh. Corina's constant anxiety! But she had to stay calm, soothing, and, above all, levelheaded.

When the bill came, Corina grabbed it. Painstakingly, she counted out peso notes.

"Thank you, Corina," both sisters said in unison.

They rose and began a slow walk back to the posada to get the car.

"Oh my," Corina said in a deeply serious voice as she shuffled along. "Do you see that?" She pointed at the scrub. "That's a desert cardinal. Soft gray-brown, tipped with a red crown and red lower face mask and underwings. A pyrrhuloxia," she said triumphantly.

They all saw it then, an unpronounceable bird perched cannily among spikes on a bush.

"Where are my binoculars? Didn't you pack them?" Corina chastised Imalia.

Kathy shot Imalia a sympathetic, conspiratorial look. Before her illness, Corina would never have treated Imalia, or anyone else for that matter, so imperiously. Despite her socialite leanings.

"Never mind," she said soothingly. "You spotted the pyrr-whatsit and it's beautiful."

Kathy wasn't that surprised that Bernard still wasn't there when they got back to the posada. As she passed reception on the way to the car, the teenager at the desk handed her an envelope. "Letter for you, Missus."

> *Kath, Went on a hike with Toby. We need time to talk about stuff later. Call me if there's news about Pete.*
> *—Bernard*

She crumpled the note. "Let's make this a short visit. I don't know about you guys, but I need to get some sleep."

And *talk about stuff later.*

CHAPTER 30

Bernard drove along the beach road for a bit, stopped for a taco, and went back to the posada. The crew had come and gone again, leaving Toby, who opted to stare at a paperback in his room, where Bernard found him and easily persuaded him to join him on the beach.

They bought beer from a stall and flopped into rented beach chairs with their respective paperbacks. But neither of them could settle. They stared at the water.

"Last night, man," Toby said eventually.

Bernard closed his book shut. "Yeah." A breeze had sprung up. It felt good on his skin.

The Sea of Cortez glittered, a Jet Ski roared by, sailboats swayed, and, far out, fishing boats roamed.

"It's never-ending, the family drama," Toby said eventually. He took another swig.

"Yeah, well, let's leave it for now, okay? You brought your phone?"

"Of course." Toby rooted around. "Shit, I must have left it in the car."

"Me too."

"What if they call?"

"I don't really feel like going there now, Tobs. Gonna go cool off." Bernard stood, stripping off his shorts, his swim trunks underneath.

"Fine by me."

Toby didn't really feel like going there either and followed Bernard into the water.

In the warm blue sea, Bernard floated on his back, letting himself drift, and, as he did, he remembered lazing just like this, way back on his honeymoon. They had driven up to Maine, hit some tourist spots, and then went inland, staying near a large freshwater lake the locals used.

A friend had told him about the place, Popham Beach. He saw three other Black people there in the five days they stayed, a family, little girl in pigtails, mom, dad. He remembered getting looks from some middle-aged white guys. Like that shit was ever going to change. It was the end of the season and hot for Maine, he recalled, but the lake water was cool, much cooler than Rincón Bay now. When he first dived into Popham Lake, he gasped at the cold, Kathy shrieking nearby. But they stayed in and got comfortable.

Kathy got a sunburn that day, and later he rubbed aloe vera into her shoulders and back at the cabin they rented, turned her over gently on the sagging bed and smoothed the cream into the parts of her breasts and stomach not covered by her bikini. He climbed on above her and they had contactless sex and it was fantastic. Her brown hair was streaked with light that summer and her face became freckled.

At Popham Beach, they got a pizza one night, and one night ate Cheerios by candlelight at the rickety table in the postage-stamp-sized kitchen, too tired from sex and sun for anything more elaborate. Then it rained one day and they drove around looking at so-called antique shops and found a big barn, filled to the rafters with books. Bernard bought a novel by a Black writer he hadn't heard of: John A. Williams. He finished the book in three days—in between fucking and swimming—and was amazed at how good Williams was. Why wasn't he up there with Baldwin and Wright? Yeah, he was that good.

When the sun came out after two days, late, it was their last day at the cabin. They went to the beach just before sunset, the only ones on that end of the lake. Kathy wanted to make love in the ocean. But Bernard said no. "Not many years ago, if they found out, they'd string me from a tree." He was in a rare mood. John A. Williams had kicked up something that had been lying still in him: Black rage transmogrified into art.

After their dip, Toby and Bernard got beers from a nearby vendor and, after Toby retrieved his phone from the car, found a beach umbrella to sit under and maybe read. But two sips in, Toby's phone rang.

He spoke briefly with Becca, then stood up. "They're letting him out," he said. "We're going home."

Bernard thought, *Let me out too.*

Dr. Maduro, the same tired woman who had been at the Unidad Familiar when they brought Pete in, informed them he was stable enough to be released, but they should get him to his own doctors right away. "Make sure he hydrates and eats these packets frequently," she added, handing them a bag of diabetic energy bars.

While Kathy and Becca took care of the paperwork, Corina and Imalia hovered in the waiting room as Bernard and Toby helped Pete, weak and shaky, into the back seat of Bernard's car, where he could lie in relative comfort. Besides, he was too tired for the force field of female energy.

As they drove, Pete soon drifted off but suddenly sat up, startled by piercingly swift sounds from the CD player. "What the hell is *that*?"

"Charlie Parker, right?" Toby, driving, guessed.

"Nope, but you're close. It's Sonny Stitt," Bernard replied triumphantly.

"Must be a clone," Toby replied in an aggrieved tone.

"But Stitt is sharper toned. Plus, no one, *no one* flies like Bird. Stitt comes close at times, I admit. That's another beer you owe me. We're doing the blindfold test," he added, turning back toward Pete. "You know, guess the musician. Or in Toby's case, stump the listener."

"F you, Bern."

"Cool," said Pete. "Can I be DJ?"

"Why not? Sure."

"I'm gonna stump you guys with this one." Pete pulled a CD from his shirt pocket and handed it to him. "Don't look."

"What, you had it in your pocket? In the hospital? Man," Bernard marveled.

"I keep this one with me at all times."

"Wow, well, let's hear it then." Bernard ejected the Stitt CD from the player and inserted Pete's CD.

After about thirty seconds of idiosyncratic rhythms and lyrics striking an uneasy balance between bluesy laments, nursery rhymes, and avant-garde knife-slash howls and swoops, Bernard cut off the player. "Okay... some kind of, uh, garage punk?"

"No, no! I know this one!" Toby pounded the dashboard. "It's... the Magic Band. Captain Beefheart. Am I right or what, Pete?"

"Nope." Pete grinned from ear to ear. "The world premiere of Peter Talley's *Stone Machone*! Get it? 'Macho' plus 'machine'!" Truthfully? Toby *was* right: it *was* an old obscure Beefheart tune but Pete *could* have written it, he reasoned. It was *his kind of thing*. Yeah. He could *easily* have come up with it. "*Stone Machone!*" he yelled.

Startled, Toby swerved sharply. Fortunately, the only other cars were in clouds of dust behind and before him.

"I impressed you that much, eh?" Pete yelled.

"Shit, Pete, I almost crashed! Don't yell like that," Toby said sharply.

"*Stone Machone!*" Pete repeated loudly.

Bernard said, "All right, all right! Let's calm down!" After a beat, he asked, "Pete, what's this about a *world premiere*?"

Pete frowned. Everybody assumed his music was all in his head, like an imaginary playmate.

"All I ask is, take care of my music after I'm gone," Pete said by way of an answer.

"Wow, what's this about?" Bernard said. "You're gonna be around for a while yet."

"Absolutely," Toby echoed.

Pete wasn't fooled. He knew phony reassurance when he heard it. But whatever. Not like he really wanted to talk about dying.

"The girls know about this *Stone Machione*?" Bernard asked.

"*Machone*. Not yet." *The girls*, Pete thought. No free ride with them. They would make it plain they didn't believe him. Always on his case. Kathy about the ice cream after he landed in that joke of a hospital, Becca beside her, shaking her head, naughty, naughty. Corina bringing up all that random shit from their childhood...

His eyes drooped. He sank into a hallucinatory swamp where his sisters were dancing around him like witches. Bitches. No, no, no! But they kept coming closer.

And then he saw with immense relief they were smiling now. He even thought he could hear them say, "We love you, Pete, love you, Pete, you, Pete."

Bernard turned to check on Pete. He was asleep and he was smiling.

"He's pretty chill now," Bernard told Toby.

"Good old Pete," Toby said loudly. "You stumped us!"

"I think he's out," Bernard said.

"Well then, it's my turn to stump the chump," Toby said. "And your turn to drive."

"Man, no, I mean, I'll drive, sure, but I will never get your rockabillies. Let me concede up front."

"*Rockabillies*?" Toby pulled the car over and stopped. They switched seats. Toby ejected Pete's CD and slid in a new one.

"No way you get to slide out of this. You roasted me, now I roast you. Fair is fair. Anyway, this first one even you will get."

They listened.

"Willie Nelson?"

"See? And now . . ." He changed CDs again.

"Oh man, what is that?" Bernard demanded. "Dude sounds like a cat with its tail in a door."

"Really, man? Really?" Toby shook his head. "You jazz snobs . . . Subtract one beer. That's Neil Young."

"Ooh, that stings, Radner," Bernard said with a chuckle.

They went back and forth like that three more times, Bernard flaming out. He didn't even get Prince.

"Game over," Toby said. "And you owe me a pitcher now. No, make that a keg."

They were making good time; not many cars were heading north. And they had managed not to discuss their wives.

Until now.

"So, what'd Becca say about your new gig?" Bernard asked after a couple of minutes.

"Oh, nothing yet—I didn't even get a chance to tell her. I'll tell her when we're back home. She's too distracted with this whole family-reunion stuff."

"What a fiasco."

"Yeah. And Kathy?"

Bernard shifted on the seat. "She, uh, remembered some more stuff from way back when she was here. It's, uh, not pretty."

"Oh man, I'm sorry. That's tough. But she's tough too; she'll get through it. She's got a lot of support. And you, of course."

"Right," said Bernard. *And all I want is a cabin in the woods.*

Pete woke up to Toby saying his name over and over. He groaned. "What? What?"

"We're back at the world-famous Burger King for a pit stop."

"Good, I gotta use the can."

It seemed to Pete that the entrance to the place was much farther away than it had been before. Then he had to walk around until he found the men's room, where he sank down onto a toilet seat and focused on his breathing. From nowhere, the words to an as-yet unwritten song came to him, right there in the funky Burger King can:

Did I hear you say
My songs are dust?
Sand it blows,
Lizards they creep,
Vultures they wheel.
Did I hear you say
I'm fool's gold?
A dried-up fool
With a brokeback guitar?
Well I'm movin' on now
I'm way beyond you

He was pleased with it. But not for long. He felt a searing pain, and then he took his last breath.

PART THREE

Six Months Later

CHAPTER 31

It was still hot at the end of October, but the days were shortening and the garden had greened up after a lot of rain; for Arizona, this was as lush as it got. Toby and Becca were eating Thai takeout on their backyard patio that could just hold the wrought-iron table and two chairs under the paloverde tree, edged by ferns, native plants, and the koi pond. When Cam had lived with them and deigned to eat with them, they'd lugged a chair out from the kitchen for him.

"This is good stuff," Toby said.

"It's from that new place."

"Cam seemed pretty upbeat today, don't you think?"

"He did."

Once a week, parents could call and talk with their boys. Cam was now living at a sober-living place in Denver.

Everything should be fine. Cam, with any luck. And they had a new car and both were busy with work, Toby making more money and Becca putting in an hour now every day before work on her poems. On the other hand, they both worried about Cam. And Becca, Toby knew, thought he was hitting the beer a little too hard.

He still hadn't been able to shake that ghastly day at the Burger King in the middle of nowhere, would never forget Bernard's face when he came back from the men's room after going to see what was taking Pete so long. Running toward him in the big, plastic dining room, shouting, "Oh my God, he's dead!" Gray with shock. The "manager," a kid who didn't know what to do, came over and Toby heard himself shout, "Call an ambulance! Call an ambulance!" and then Bernard saying, "We gotta tell the girls," rubbing his face as if trying to remove the traces of what he'd seen. "They're gonna freak, Toby!"

But the Talley women did not freak, at least not outwardly, when, fifteen minutes later, they got to the fast-food restaurant. They went still and huddled together solemnly as the EMTs and police appeared and Pete's covered body was wheeled out on its way to the morgue in Tucson. Except for Corina, who kept asking what happened; Becca and Kathy and Imalia took turns explaining to her. And then it seemed maybe a little obscene to order drinks to go from Burger King, but they all did after Pete had been removed. The manager wouldn't charge them. Then they drove the rest of the way home.

That was months ago but Toby still had nightmares about it. Sometimes he dreamed that it was Cam who had died. Becca had suggested several times that maybe he should "talk to someone," but Toby hadn't taken her up on that. He felt he just needed time to work his way out of what he knew was a fragile state.

"We need to talk," Bernard said, appearing in the doorway of Kathy's studio.

"Now? Can we do it after my meeting? I can't skip Border Aid tonight; we have a lot of organizing to do for the new shelter." *Does anyone*, she thought, *hear those words, 'we need to talk,' without their heart sinking?* And it was the second time in a week he'd said it. But she was behind in everything. There had been so much to do after Pete died, and it wasn't done yet. "Why don't I pick up dinner after the meeting and we can talk then? From that new Mediterranean place?"

"Fine," Bernard said, and he left, presumably to his desk in the bedroom.

Kathy found the piece of paper she'd been looking for, then remembered she hadn't called Corina in two days. She picked up her cell phone—it would have to be a quick call.

But it was Becca who answered Corina's phone.

"Hey, I was just going to call you. I'm at her house. More shit! She ran away again. Last night, Kathy! In the middle of the night! Thank God, some neighbors recognized her, all the way at the end of the road, by the foothills! Barefoot! They brought her home. Juana—you know, the new housekeeper? She called me a little while ago, so I'm with her now. I called her doctor—the shrink—Kathy, she's a mess. Please, can you come over?"

So Kathy went to Corina's, where she and Becca spent the rest of the day on the phone with some home health aide agencies that Dr. Lorber's receptionist had recommended. Round-the-clock care was not easy to find and incredibly expensive, but Corina could afford it. Eventually, they managed to line up two women for interviews, then sat with Corina—perfectly calm now. Juana made some sandwiches. Finally, Kathy had to leave to make the Border Aid meeting.

Her head throbbed as she drove there.

It was a long meeting. She knew she should stay for the whole thing, but she kept thinking about Bernard's "we need to talk," and after an hour and a half, she told a colleague that she had a family matter she had to deal with. And well, she did, didn't she?

"God, what a shitstorm," she said, coming into the townhouse. "Corina..."

Bernard was watching a tennis match. "Uh-huh," he said. "Got the food?"

"Oh shit, I forgot. I'm sorry, I just wanted to get home and—"

He heaved himself up from the couch. "Guess I'll scramble up some huevos rancheros then."

"Hey, I am sorry."

Half an hour later, Bernard had prepared the eggs, refried beans, tortillas, and a green salad. "Food's ready," he called. No response.

He stuck his head into the living room. Kathy was stretched out on the couch, sound asleep.

"Right," he said, "what else is new." He went back to the kitchen, removed a portion of the dinner for Kathy to heat up later, and took a tray to his desk in the bedroom. He planned to review the afternoon's work on the last chapter while he ate. Instead of that, he stared out the window and thought about last weekend. They had finally finished going through the last dregs of stuff they had thrown in bin bags from Pete's apartment and stored in Corina's voluminous garage for the time being. Kathy had tackled most of it—old cassettes, CDs, and junk mail, mostly. Or rather, Kathy had said she would go through the stuff, but she was atypically inefficient, dithering, staring into space. She had been like that since the trip. Not surprising: she had those recovered memories to deal with, Pete's demise, and Corina going down the tubes.

Bernard was still taking it hard too. Finding Pete like that. He hadn't been able to focus much on the book. What helped was knowing that he'd lined up a little place in Prescott for the long winter break. It wasn't that far from the Grand Canyon; maybe he'd go hiking there.

He watched the sunset around the foothills fade from lavender-pink to silver. *I'm going to miss the view*, he thought. He knew it in every shade of light and dark, those elephantine, ancient shapes that loomed as if eternally on the horizon. And the tall saguaros on the plain, standing like sentinels. As a little boy, Theo had been afraid of saguaro cacti—saw them as giants who could come after him.

Kathy spoke his name and touched his shoulder.

Bernard wheeled around. "Whoa!" he exclaimed.

"Hey! Didn't mean to startle you. The door was open, so I . . . just wanted to thank you. For making dinner. Delicious, as always."

"Glad you liked it." He felt his heart seem to close with a thump, like slamming a heavy book shut. God, it hurt.

"Bernard, what do you want to talk about? 'Cause I know we haven't had a chance to much. With . . . everything that's happened."

He was motionless in his chair as she thumped down on the bed.

"Look, I—"

"This isn't working anymore, is it." Not a question, a statement of fact.

He shook his head. "No. It's not."

She put her head in her hands.

God, he thought, *I hate this. Hurting her.* "In January, I thought I'd rent this little cabin I found. Up in Prescott. For the winter break. Actually, I have rented it. And find, you know, a place when I get back."

"So you've already decided." Kathy sprang up, shaking her head wildly. "Wow. And you said nothing about it? We don't, we don't . . . do things like that. Without talking to each other."

"When was I supposed to talk to you? You're always at some meeting or dealing with some crisis with your family."

There was Wi-Fi there, he'd made sure of that. It was just a one-room place, but a good-sized room, with a fireplace, galley kitchen, and a cubbyhole of a bathroom. He couldn't wait to get there. "I've got to finish the book," he added.

"Oh, the *book*. Of course. That's what matters." But she spoke without bitterness. Which somehow made this conversation even harder than he'd expected.

Kathy sat quietly then for a long moment, remembering the night he'd told her about the affair he'd been having. Six, seven years ago?

They'd had dinner and the kids were asleep or at least in bed with the lights off. In the old house, bursting at the seams with two adults and two teenagers. For some reason, she remembered, she and Bernard were going to watch some show. Something she was really looking forward to. But before she could click it on, Bernard blurted out that he'd been having an affair but it was all over now. Just like that.

When she could formulate speech, she asked him if it with was a student. And he said, well, yes, but a mature student. Kathy had met her, he said. At some department function.

"Oh, well, if it's a *mature student*," she said. That was supposed to make it less egregious? "Does this mature student have a name?"

"Sondra Bowen. You chatted for a few minutes, I think, at the Christmas party."

"Oh yes, the Christmas party." And she remembered a tall, dark, lean woman—her opposite, in fact. Who had mentioned she was just finishing her thesis and "Professor Talley" had been "a big help." But what did she look like? No image came to mind. Well, she'd have to have been reasonably good-looking for Bernard to—

"She told me you were a big help with her thesis," Kathy said as if on autopilot and found then that she was throwing at him the first thing that came to hand: a copy of *The Journal of Jazz Studies*. It grazed his cheek and fell to the floor. "A big help!" Kathy yelled, standing up. She found she was trembling and making odd noises. Crying?

"I'm sorry. Kath, I'm so sorry, I never meant—"

"You're just like Tom Swanson. A fucking cheat."

"I am not like him. It was—"

Kathy shrieked, sank to the floor, and willed the tears to stop. After a few moments, a lifetime, she said, "What do you mean you're not like him? You are like him."

Then Bernard walked out. She figured he'd gone to Toby and Becca's and slept on their couch. The next morning, she called and asked him to come home. So they could talk.

She remembered the curious feeling she had that next morning when he walked in, as if she were very light, almost airborne, as if she were separating from her physical mass. At the same time, she wanted to punch him.

Bernard again said he was sorry, that Sondra Bowen had left town, she had lined up a teaching job in the Midwest, Ohio or Michigan. Then he said it would never happen again.

"If she'd stayed here, you'd still be fucking her, though?" But she felt her anger fading. Because of a niggling, oh so inconvenient fact: she too had been unfaithful, though she had never told him. So long ago. A one-night stand, a stupid fling like she used to have before she met Bernard. Except it happened two years after they were married, *happily* married, when they were in Manhattan for a summer, had sublet an apartment. She was always going to galleries back then, mostly shabby storefront shows on the Lower East Side or Brooklyn, when those places were grungy, often dangerous, not yet pronounced cool. Usually, she went with Bernard or a friend, but this one night she was on her own. And yes, she'd had a couple of glasses of wine, but she wasn't high. She couldn't blame it on that. She just wanted to forget she was married, feel single again, beholden to no one. And it felt good by the second glass of wine. There was this guy, tall, thin, with beautiful blond hair down his back. He was witty, he was attractive. They went to another gallery, had another glass of wine, and ended up at his apartment. It was when they were making love on a futon—well, fucking—that she knew she'd made a mistake. The guy fell asleep and she left. She had to walk for blocks before she found a cab to take her to the Upper West Side. She didn't care how dangerous it was. Maybe deep down she wanted to be punished. Her little fantasy of being on her own and unencumbered had quickly imploded and she was disgusted with herself. And not long after that, she heard through the grapevine that the guy was bisexual. They'd had unprotected sex and it was when the AIDS plague was starting to roar, so she lived in silent terror about her status, putting off lovemaking with Bernard with lies about a very stubborn and painful yeast infection until she learned she'd been spared.

Bernard's affair was payback.

"Are you fucking somebody else?" she asked now, six years after his affair, unable to stop herself. "Is that what this is about?"

Bernard shook his head. "Shit, Kathy."

She believed him. "I can't imagine living here by myself. Without you."

"You'll be all right. Everybody needs you."

"You mean everybody *else*!" she shouted.

CHAPTER 32

It was not a car she was in, Kathy realized, but a hearse. And it was moving too fast. She watched the sea whip by. Abruptly, she saw the desert stretch on every side. In the middle of nowhere, the hearse drove past a rudimentary cemetery dotted with wooden crosses and sticks that she knew were the graves of people who had died trying to cross the border. But why, she wondered, didn't the hearse stop? It was carrying a body to be buried, wasn't it? And this was the place. Immediately the dream shifted, and Kathy knew she was walking in a park in Tucson, in fact the park where Pete had collapsed outside that Black Lives Matter rally. Then she realized the hearse had deposited her there with an urn that was all that was left of Pete. Just then a figure ran by, wearing the black, old-fashioned mourning of long ago. Or was it a burka? No, a hoodie, in fact, and the figure was Bernard.

As she called out to him to stop, Kathy woke up.

He should have a hangover, be exhausted, but Bernard felt the buoyancy of relief. They'd both had to work yesterday, but

Kathy had agreed to talk that evening, or at least she hadn't said no. But last night they'd ended up arguing again—shouted at each other in fact, and then tried to be reasonable as they drank two bottles of wine, which was a bottle more than usual. Here were the empties on the coffee table next to the couch where he'd fallen asleep—okay, passed out. Kathy must still be asleep in the bedroom.

He got up, made coffee, toast, and took a tray into the bedroom. Least he could do. But when he opened the door, she wasn't there. Had she woken up in the middle of the night and gone to Becca's or Corina's, still smashed? Or gotten up early for one of her endless meetings? He wondered if she would tell her sisters. What would she tell them? And Toby, of course. He wondered where he would stay. There was November and December to get through. He just couldn't do this anymore. Tonight he'd sleep in his office, grim but doable. Then he'd get an Airbnb, or a sublet until January.

He began to pack, throwing clothes in a duffel. He got his shaving kit, his toothbrush. He wondered, again, if he was some kind of monster. But he felt freer than he had in a long time.

He abandoned his packing, drawn like a magnet to his laptop, the penultimate pages of *Without Walls*. For once, the unblinking gaze of the unseen audience—the critics, the academy—was unimportant. Beside the point. *Do I finally not give a shit?* he wondered. He had a slight headache, but he was loose, limber, focused on the business at hand. And old enough to know he might not feel this way too often again. But that didn't matter; all that mattered was that he was coming to the finish line. Good reviews, bad reviews, none of that seemed to matter anymore. Because soon he would be done. And he'd no longer be living with the woman he knew better than anyone in the world but who had never let him in completely.

He wrote—well, he thought—until hunger drove him to the kitchen.

After a second cup of coffee and a sliced banana ("Why do you always slice them?" Kathy had asked when they were getting to know each other, in another lifetime, and he'd shrugged; it was like that with most everything: just the way it was), Bernard pondered the day before him. Would she be willing to talk sensibly to him soon? They would have to do that. Or, what if she happened to come home now, found him here; would she demand that he leave immediately? He should go for one last run up to the foothills, take advantage of the relative coolness of the morning. This might be his last opportunity—Jesus! But he only moved from his desk to the couch, half sitting, half lying. Now that he was going, he found he wanted to linger.

The Bird and The Wolf, he thought. *That's how I'll always think of the book, the title within the title.* It came to him then that he also thought of it as *A Boy and His Father*. That other lone wolf, his father.

In the afterword that had become the last chapter after what he thought was the ending—the chapter he didn't know he was going to write until he had to—he would describe those master classes in the cramped living room in West Orange, New Jersey. Young Bernard wanted to be out playing ball, climbing trees, messing around, but, thumbing through his records, Senior would be telling him, "Here's a giant, too much going on for a boy in short pants yet," holding up something by Hindemith or Ellington. "But we'll get there. Now, sit down, listen to this." Then some James P. Johnson, some Fats Waller. His father had exposed him in time to the intricacies of Lunceford, Chopin, the Twelve Clouds of Joy, Mendelssohn, Machito, Bach, Art Tatum, Monk, Mary Lou Williams, Schumann, Charlie Parker, in no particular order. Those records had been his real education, the music of the world's people, and the people he came from as an integral part of the world's musical warp and weave. It had kept him from the streets, from the familiar fate of so many of his classmates: the neighborhood, the ongoing servitude of drugs, guns, incarceration, even death. It had also made him weird, a loner. Nobody his age cared about the music he did, cared about what it meant. The cruel irony: that even in Black America, Black creativity was largely ignored, demeaned, misunderstood, and always, always monetized.

Senior layered the outrages of their people into his musical tutorials, in mostly cryptic but telling comments that punctuated the sounds. So that slowly, young Bernard became aware of the great uprootedness of that far continent, the Africa re-rooted in stony ground that had dug down deep, thriving despite neglect and dishonor. He discovered that this *African American origin music* was a trickster, the origin heartbeat rhythms shape-shifting and insinuating, blooming as lushly in the cracks of sidewalks and garbage-strewn vacant lots of Black people's enforced living conditions as in the well-tended gardens of a Euro-American mansion. Black creativity might be treated largely as an invasive weed by the establishment, but it knew not just how to survive. It thrived.

Bernard felt the familiar trills and tom-toms of heritage anger, and he thought, *I'm writing about reclamation acclamation elation.*

Then he thought, *Maybe I'm still a little drunk from last night.*

In his mind, he saw his father holding up a fist. And smiling.

CHAPTER 33

"Amalia! Where are you! I keep calling you, but you don't come!" Corina's voice rose to a shriek from her bedroom.

Groggily, Kathy ran to her sister. The previous night, she'd walked out of the house. She had to get away from Bernard before she did something she'd regret, like smash a frying pan over his head where he lay snoring on the sofa. No matter how satisfying it might be in the short term. She'd realized after throwing some things into an overnight bag and getting in the car that she was not exactly sober—in fact, she'd had to squint against passing headlights like the old lady with cataracts she would doubtless become if she were lucky to live that long— and that she was heading for Corina's house, where she'd sleep uneasily in one of the spare bedrooms. (But better that than being in her own bed and knowing her husband, partner, former soulmate, was in the same house. Or having to deal with Becca and Toby's mute questions if she showed up at theirs in the middle of the night.)

"You?" Corina queried now. "But where's Imalia?"

"Imalia doesn't work here anymore, remember? Juana does. But she won't be here until eight."

"Well, it's time for breakfast."

"It's only six thirty," Kathy started to point out but then thought better of it. "Oh well, come on, I'll make us something." Soon, thank God, there would be someone staying with Corina overnight.

She led Corina to the kitchen and set about making coffee and toast and cutting slices of cantaloupe. Corina sat with her head bowed.

"I want to tell you something," she said suddenly, just as Kathy put the food down in front of her.

"Sure. What?"

"Pete had *guns* in his house." Kathy waited, open-mouthed, as Corina chewed a bite of toast very slowly. "Dad's old army rifle and another one. I found them in the hall closet."

"Guns? Shit, were they loaded? And why am I not that surprised?" She paused a beat, let the news settle. "Wait, we didn't find any guns when we cleaned out his apartment."

"Because *I* found them, oh . . . a while back. Then he got mad at me, the way he does."

"Did," Kathy said gently.

"He says they're . . . souvenirs. But I took them to the trash bins while he was sleeping."

"Corina, did this really happen?"

"You don't believe me."

"Um, sure I do. Well, Pete had some dark places."

In one of those flashes of her old self, Corina said fiercely, "Well, who doesn't? Have some dark places?"

The front door opened. Juana bustled in, a sturdy woman of indeterminate age. She went straight to the lockbox on a shelf in the kitchen and got some of the all-important meds. "It's time for your pills, Mrs. Corina."

Kathy took Juana aside. "She's upset today."

Juana had cared for Alzheimer's patients before. She nodded. "Every morning before she takes her meds. Then she calms down. Usually. Till later in the afternoon. Bad time then."

Kathy felt the familiar stab of guilt for not visiting Corina more often. Excuses. But it was the second-hardest thing she had ever done, be there for her sister as she lost her mind, and there were times she came up with every conceivable reason not to go.

"That's when they get really agitated," Juana went on. "Cry, yell, walk and walk around in little circles . . ."

"I wish I could be here more," Kathy said, feeling spineless.

"You are all busy." Juana shrugged. "And sometimes, she's worse after you come. She doesn't want to be by herself."

This, Kathy could understand.

As Toby drank another beer, he stared at the koi languidly traversing their tiny water world. He hadn't been able to sleep, so he had been out in the backyard and now it was, like, the middle of the night, which was marginally cooler than the three-digit heat of recent days. He wondered if the fish were affected by the high temperatures, though they spent plenty on bags of ice for the pond.

For the first time, he wished he hadn't gotten the full-time job at the U. It was locking him in, like a vise. Plus, he always felt like pulling up stakes and driving north where there was some kind of fall foliage by this time of year in Arizona. At first, he hadn't missed the four seasons of the Northeast—was simply euphoric, like any new transplant, at missing winter—but now he felt, well, *cooked*. But he was stuck here, wasn't he?

They had argued earlier about Cam again. He'd half hoped that Becca, with all those Al-Anon meetings behind her, would have been freed of the slime pit of parental guilt, shame, fear, and anger around their son. She still worried, stressed herself out, even ranted at times, but she'd also been functioning well and she'd been notified that one of her poems had been accepted for publication—a minor journal but one she admired. Toby thought she'd be thrilled. And maybe she would have been, but then Cam had called from his brand-new sober residence place in Denver, insisting he had to have a car to get to his job—his first, part-time, minimum-wage job as a stock boy in a grocery store—and Becca told him no, he could take the bus, and he'd screamed abuse at her and hung up.

She held on to this news until they were eating their grilled turkey burgers in the backyard. Maybe she expected Toby to commiserate—and yeah, he was sorry, of course, that she'd had to take shit from Cam, but he was also pissed off that, once again, she'd made a decision without him.

"You don't even ask me what I think about getting him a car? He could have at least looked into used cars. But no. Well, I'm his father; I have a say in this too."

"He only calls when he wants something. And then you cave," she said.

"Don't make this about me!"

"Well, it *is* about you. Cam knows just how to play you. He wants money for stuff now that he's at that sober-living place, and you give it to him. A new laptop? A new phone? A car? Oh, snap. Doesn't matter that we're just starting to get out of debt. You still cave."

Toby drooped a little over the remains of the meal on his plate. "I don't always cave, Becca."

Becca burst out crying. She usually wasn't a crier, but since Pete had died, she'd been doing it fairly often. She managed to say, "For ten years I've been supporting this family."

Toby's head snapped up. "I pull my weight."

Flinging him a dark look, she marched out of the back yard and went upstairs to their bedroom, all but slamming the door.

He'd thought about going out, dropping by the Freakness to clear his head. But he didn't want to be one of those pathetic middle-aged guys huddled on a barstool. It wasn't the same without Bernard, but Bernard kept saying he had to finish the book, he'd be in touch when it was done.

Bernard had pretty much avoided him, he realized, since what they mutually called "the disaster." And Toby wondered if Bernard and Kathy were going to separate. They seemed to just barely tolerate each other, the few times he'd seen them. And yeah, sure, he thought about it too. Of course he did, and he assumed Becca did too. What married couple didn't? He was angry, but they'd work through it, he and Becca. Once she got over herself.

CHAPTER 34

As Kathy was driving downtown the next morning, a Saturday, she thought about the day before. She had been at Corina's until she had to go teach at the community college and then home for one more round with Bernard. The awkwardness of it, the boxes of books, records, and CDs, packed and lined up by the front door, final proof. He hadn't heard her come in, and when she saw the expression on his face—just flat, done—she wanted to sink to the floor and smack him, all at the same time. "I'll have all my stuff out of here tomorrow," he'd said. He'd lucked out right away, found a studio at a good price.

A truck pulled out suddenly in front of her and she had to slam on the brakes. "Fuck!" she yelled. Yes, double *fuck*. Was it her fault he was leaving? Kathy the fixer, the rescuer. The shoeless shoemaker, the sick physician . . .

She started shaking and had to pull over on the shoulder. "Fuck!" she yelled again, pounding her hands on the steering wheel, and suddenly the thought of her mother's face if she could hear her now made her laugh, her proper mother who had once actually wiped a bar of soap across her mouth after she banged her big toe on a chair leg when she was in, like, eighth grade and said, "Shit." Had Corina and Becca had their mouths washed out with soap? Pete? Probably every day from the time he was out of diapers.

She had to park several blocks from the large main library, her destination. Downtown Tucson was busier now than it used to be, and parking was accordingly harder to find and no longer free. She pulled into a lot, paid, and walked two blocks to the Joel D. Valdez library, which also looked like a parking garage.

Inside, a tweedy man with, she thought idly, the kind of nondescript face that would make him a perfect spy—who really notices a librarian?—guided her through the process of using the antiquated microfiche machine, since the newspapers she wanted to look at had not been digitized. "Blame the legislature," he added in a not-convincing joking aside about the stingy old coots still mostly ruling Arizona.

She hand-cranked the thing to scroll through a stream of old, yellowed newsprint, looking for any mention of a young woman whose first name started with *J* sometime in April of 1986, the exact date long vanished from her memory. Social media had yielded nothing about a rape/murder/attack/death on the beach at Rincón Bay back then. Stone-age technology was her last chance.

She pictured finding a front page with headlines like "TUCSON U STUDENT DISAPPEARS IN RINCÓN BAY DURING SPRING BREAK BACCHANAL," OR "SEARCH ON FOR MISSING U OF AZ STUDENT IN RINCÓN BAY," OR (PLEASE, GOD, NO) "TUCSON STUDENT FOUND SLAIN ON MEXICAN BEACH," OR (PLEASE,

God, yes) "tucson student found alive on mexican beach."

Or perhaps "man blinded in attack on beach" or "man found slain on beach."

Even with the glass screen that protected the fragile newsprint, Kathy breathed in the dust of decades as she moved through page after page. But she found nothing about an assault on a young American woman whose name started with J or any other letter, or a Mexican or American man wounded or mortally wounded for that matter, in Rincón Bay at that time.

Hunched over the archaic machine, Kathy waited for the sweet swell of relief. If "something had happened" to J, wouldn't there have been a report about it in the news? So the lack of news had to mean J was okay. Didn't it? J, she hoped, wanted to think, had gotten lots of therapy—trauma being the thing now. Had rebuilt her life. And the fact that she'd found nothing about any men or boys in the obits of the paper told Kathy that her attacker was not—yes, she could finally say it, thank you, Anne—dead. Possibly one-eyed. With an eye patch like a pirate, a memento of his crime. But not dead. But wait: Maybe J had been badly hurt but hadn't reported it. Or worse, she had gone to the authorities and they either did nothing or tried to extort a bribe or both. It was Mexico. It was possible.

The doubts were always whispering to her. Anne had warned her about the controversy over recovered memories. But Kathy felt sure the details she now remembered—the quick struggle, the stab to the eye of her attacker with the room key, J's screams—were accurate. What she couldn't remember, would probably never remember, was if she had alerted anybody to J's situation. She'd had to live with that for so long. And would continue to have to.

But a voice in Kathy's head—Anne's?—said sometimes the choice is between saving yourself or someone else.

When she got back in the car, Kathy felt an unfamiliar lightness. For so long she had been terrified of what she had done, and what she had not done, on the beach at Rincón Bay. She had gone on to take care of others—grains in the sand of misery, maybe, but what more could she do? In the process, though, somehow she had lost the person dearest to her, her soulmate. And it was classic—she got that now, he'd made sure that she had—that the love of her life had felt ignored, taken for granted.

She had persuaded herself that she must be there for others, but she hadn't been there for him.

Now it was time to take care of herself.

She bent her head and sobbed. It felt good.

CHAPTER 35

Everything outdoors pretty much stopped with the summer heat. When the temperature reached above 105 or so, people who worked outside switched to a night schedule and the rest of the world stayed indoors. But Kathy couldn't remember it lasting so long. It was almost Christmas again; Bernard had been gone for more than a year. How, she wondered, did all the climate-change deniers in Arizona square that with reality? She was busy, though, and pushed through the heat like it was still August. At night, aside from Border Aid meetings, Kathy had time to deep clean the townhouse, work on her paintings. She went to Chicago to visit Tamara, in her second year of grad school at Northwestern. At home, Theo came by most Sundays.

In September, she'd started teaching again, including another class at Lola's Cantina, some of the same women from the previous class and several newcomers. They did life studies. Nora was still working at the bar part-time, she told Kathy, while she and Imalia were renovating the bottom floor of an old building for the coffeehouse they were calling Norima's. They hoped to open it by the new year.

Nora agreed to model for the class. Draped against the bar wearing only a long pink feathery scarf around her sturdy hips with the ends thrown back over a shoulder that was strongly molded from thousands of years of carrying heavy jugs and bundles, she seemed at ease with displaying the marks of her life, the furrows, creases, and scars on her coffee-brown skin. When Kathy called time, Nora threw up her arms and stretched and the class applauded. Afterward, the women chatted lightheartedly, like the girls they had probably never been allowed to be. Certainly, Kathy was sure, they had not imagined using crayons, ink pens, watercolors, and poster paints to make images of a naked woman.

Later, back at the townhouse, Kathy resumed working on her own portrait of Nora. She was planning a new series, all the students at Lola's, ranging in age from their twenties to their sixties.

After she worked for a while, she went to the kitchen, idly contemplating making a meal. It was so quiet. Maybe too quiet. But Theo was coming over later; he said he had something to tell her. The kids knew that their parents were "taking a break." Would Theo confront her about specifics?

Kathy had called Bernard earlier in the week. "I don't know why you are so reluctant to tell your children about the divorce, since you've moved out for good, but if you don't tell them this week, I will," she'd begun, without preliminaries.

Of course things had gone downhill from there.

"Until we're *sure*?" she yelled. "I'm supposed to wait around for you to decide? Well, I'm sure," she'd told him. And hung up.

After staring into the refrigerator, she caved and poured her go-to bowl of granola, adding some blueberries and turning on the radio as she ate at the kitchen island. It was set to Bernard's favorite station, jazz and blues and R & B. She recognized the sexy tune playing and the pianist—"Señor Blues" by Horace Silver. She'd heard it often; it was on one of Bernard's LPs. He'd taken some of them with him to his new place, but most of them were still stacked here in the corner of the kitchen. Of course, he probably hadn't any room for them there, but she resented their presence.

She finished the granola and was about to turn off the radio when the unmistakable sound of Bernard's idol, Charlie Parker, came on, playing "If I Should Lose You," a pretty tune from long ago that, true to form, Bird blew to gold.

As the song came to an end, Becca called, and immediately after hanging up with her, Kathy called Theo.

Her son kept telling her to text, that voicemails were "old-school." Uncharacteristically, today he picked up on the second ring.

"Mom, I'm at work, what?"

"I'm really sorry, Theo, I'm going to have to cancel our dinner tonight. We'll do it soon, yeah?"

"Shit, I wanted you to meet Bill. We're moving in together, Mom! Okay, well Sunday's good for us. Can Dad maybe do a barbecue? Oops, sorry, I forgot."

"Anyway, he's trying to finish the book."

"What else is new?"

"The publisher gave him a deadline." For Bernard had just signed a contract with Cal.

"Right, but can't he even do like a Sunday dinner?"

Kathy was silent. She wanted to tell him that they were going to get a divorce in person, not on the phone.

"Mom, why don't you guys just cut the cord already? Jesus."

"Oh, Theo . . . Yes. We're going to."

"God, you've split for good and you don't even *tell* me? Did you tell Tamara? You and her are always having those deep conversations and leaving me out of everything. Wow, this is fucked-up, I can't believe it."

"Theo, stop! Just stop. These things are messy . . . Look, I do want to meet . . . Bill. And see you, of course. And your father and I will talk to you about . . . things. Just not tonight."

"Okay, we'll do takeout," Theo, who was essentially a happy soul, said more calmly.

"I can manage the grill."

"Mom, no, you suck at that. Otherwise," he added hastily, "you're perfect."

"Well, thank you, Theo."

"You sound kinda down. Well, you would be."

"A little, I guess. And also your aunt . . . she's having issues."

"She's lucky she's got you and Aunt Becs."

"Thanks, Thee. Okay then, see you Sunday. And, I'm fine, don't worry about me."

Earlier that day, Corina had slipped and fallen. Again. She wasn't hurt, just bruised, but that's what Becca had called about. They'd both gotten the texts from Juana earlier. Becca had said she was going over, asked her to come too.

Kathy had agreed, of course.

It was nearly dusk when Kathy got to Corina's. She'd stopped first at the little Mexican place she liked to get fish tacos—plain for Corina, no spices, nada. Some guac and chips.

Becca's car was already there. Just as well. Becca was calmer, handled Corina better.

At least it wasn't fiercely hot anymore. Just hot. What if she turned around and went to Bernard's apartment complex? *Surprise! It's me, honey!* Or no, what if she drove north, went to the Grand Canyon, lost herself in its beauty. Found a town she liked and just put down new roots, found a job as a bartender. Hooked up with a tall, rangy guy who screwed the hell out of her and had nothing much to say. Heaven.

The gravel crunched in the semicircle in front of Corina's house as Kathy drove up. Her gaze drifted over the expensive, well-tended varieties of cacti and flowering shrubs she had never learned the names of. She breathed slowly, turned off the engine, and thought, *If Corina's calmed down, we can eat out on the patio. Watch old Henrique bulldoze along the zoysia grass at 0.0000005 miles an hour, the hummers that dart like colorful bullets to the feeders, and then the night critters, bats flitting, coyotes creeping. Just be together while we can.*

She went into the house and hugged her sisters.

ABOUT THE AUTHOR

Geoffrey Doughlin

Linda Dahl began writing as a freelancer about two passions, jazz and Latin America, before turning to fiction. She has written ten published books, including the novels *Tiny Vices, An Upside-Down Sky, Gringa in a Strange Land,* and *The Bad Dream Notebook,* and the nonfiction works *Stormy Weather* and *Morning Glory.* Her books have consistently garnered awards and praise, including a Notable Book of the Year nod from *The New York Times Book Review* for *Morning Glory* in 2000. Linda loves reading, swimming, music, and doing volunteer work in her community. She lives in Riverdale, New York.

Looking for your next great read?

We can help!

Visit www.shewritespress.com/next-read
or scan the QR code below for a list
of our recommended titles.

She Writes Press is an award-winning
independent publishing company founded to
serve women writers everywhere.